BLOODY HELL!

Other titles by Roy (Toby) Bishop:

Cry Havoc : *A Trip To Hell for a Group of Ageing Mercenaries Who Should Have Known Better* (ISBN: 0-595-32165-8)

A Debt of Honour (ISBN: 0-595-38837-X)

Sold to Evil (iUniverse, 2006)

More information at
www.diadembooks.com/bishop.htm

BLOODY HELL!

An Ex-Soldier's Experience in West Africa after 30 Years in the British Army

Major Roy Edward Bishop, MBE (known as Toby)

To: Scott

with best wishes.

R. B......... (Toby).

14th November 2009.

iUniverse, Inc.
New York Lincoln Shanghai

BLOODY HELL!

Copyright © 2004, 2006 by Roy Edward Bishop

All rights reserved. No part of this book may be used or reproduced by any means, graphic, electronic, or mechanical, including photocopying, recording, taping or by any information storage retrieval system without the written permission of the publisher except in the case of brief quotations embodied in critical articles and reviews.

iUniverse books may be ordered through booksellers or by contacting:

iUniverse
2021 Pine Lake Road, Suite 100
Lincoln, NE 68512
www.iuniverse.com
1-800-Authors (1-800-288-4677)

ISBN-13: 978-0-595-32538-2 (pbk)
ISBN-13: 978-0-595-82333-8 (cloth)
ISBN-13: 978-0-595-77335-0 (ebk)
ISBN-10: 0-595-32538-6 (pbk)
ISBN-10: 0-595-82333-5 (cloth)
ISBN-10: 0-595-77335-4 (ebk)

Printed in the United States of America

This book is dedicated to my family for their understanding when I left the Army to become a private contractor; perhaps they thought it would be my first step towards normality after so long in H M Forces.

To Frederick Bran and Frank Bourne, who inspired me to do what I have done—I did not let them down.

To Colonel Brian Rawlings and my friends from the 4th Guards Brigade days, who gave me the second kick-start I needed in life.

To the people of Ghana from whom I learnt a great deal about myself, I owe a debt of gratitude—especially to the wise old "greybeards" who spoke of the past and their hopes for the future. I even forgive whoever nicked my only pair of scissors and my blackthorn cane.

Contents

Foreword ix
Prologue 1
THE WAR YEARS 5
THE EARLY YEARS AFTER THE WAR 10
THE BRITISH ARMY 1956–1986 15
PROJECT 3072 37
WHAT HAVE I DONE? 39
GHANA 43
AKUSE—MY VILLAGE 46
THE BUNGALOW 49
RECRUITING AND TRAINING THE NEW SECURITY
    FORCE 52
HOLIDAY AND A RAPE 79
THE CHAPEL IN THE BUSH 82
VISITORS 85
THE FRIGHTENED GIRL 89
THE PIG 92
LEISURE TIME 96
THE DRUMS 102

A TRIP TO THE SEASIDE.............................. 105
THE CHIEF'S PARTY................................. 108
THE WHITE BABY.................................... 112
THE DEAD MAN 114
THE CHILDREN ARE SILENT........................... 116
THE LAKE VISIT 118
Epilogue 121

Foreword

This is a tale of the experiences and opinions of a former army officer (seeking to change his way of life) after thirty years serving in H M Forces. The total change from a regulated and controlled military establishment to that of working in isolation in West Africa, without communication, and with limited support from the outside world, came as a shock—and he had to deal with it. The challenge was to train a security force for the Volta River Authority. The threat was the fear of sabotage to their power-producing hydro electric dams and major theft of essential items of expensive equipment, which was difficult to replace as any interruption of the power supply would not only affect Ghana but neighbouring countries to whom it was sold.

This account tells how Roy Bishop, ill prepared and poorly equipped, came to terms with this adventure, and how the people and the land affected him and gradually changed his knowledge of himself and life. The tale starts with the birth and early days of the man at the end of the war and the dangers faced in Kent from bombing and the V1 Doodlebug rockets, the hardship of his family's farm life and his joining the army in 1956, and then progresses through a summary of his army career with stories from many parts of the world when he took the major decision to change his lifestyle completely and take a private contract in Ghana.

The bulk of the story illustrates the challenges, trials and amusing incidents throughout the year's stay in Ghana—situations or incidents which today, in the time of the mobile phone, could not have happened, but did in 1986. For those interested in Africa and the activity of private contract men working in this dark continent, the story will surely be fascinating. Magic Ju Ju, the poverty of the people, the savagery of some, the loyalty and the friendship of others, make up this collection of tales within the story. This was a lesson in life.

The theme is that when you go to play in Africa, be sure to take only what you can afford to lose—and that does not mean your life!

Prologue

It has taken me some time to record a part of my life that I feel would be of interest to any ex-serviceman, anyone who has lived and worked in Africa and those who will find these accounts perhaps different from the many blood-and-guts stories based upon the continent's turbulent history as it dragged itself into the 20th century. It has been a land of exploration, exploitation and the graveyard of many who have tried to tame this black motherland with its huge diversity of peoples, climate and the untold wealth it still offers. If I had not chanced upon the opportunity to work in West Africa I would have missed the chance to experience life at its most basic and the education of the life and hardships of the people of Ghana.

I hope I can convey the surprise, shock and bewildering time I had in the early days after my arrival and how I slowly fitted in with my neighbours and indeed enjoyed their company and well-deserved respect. Most people who write about Africa are pro-white or pro-black. I was neither, though it's true that I might have been a bit racist at home—but that was born out of ignorance. The first black man I saw was in Kent; John was the head butler for a wealthy landowner who had farmed in East Africa and when he came to the UK, John came back with him. He was a tall, fine-featured man who dressed immaculately and always had his day off on a Friday. John had his favourite pub and on his night off the locals always ensured that he had his half hour slot to gamble on the one-armed bandit machine. Had I known it, this was the type of friendship and acceptance I was to experience some thirty years later, the theme being: 'Treat people as you would wish to be treated yourself.' Good manners are the strongest weapon.

The start of my tales gives a humorous insight into my army career. I have deliberately left out a lot of sadness because that's not the theme of this book. It will show how ill prepared I was to cope with the shocks I had, and the blame for this I place on those who sent me and those who would be with me. As an ex-professional soldier, perhaps I should have made a better analysis myself, but the contract did say accommodation and a telephone. (What bloody telephone!)

Retiring from the Army in early 1986 I entered into the world of 'civvy street'. I was completely innocent in many ways and this would prove to be the basis for a lot of my problems that I encountered. There was a vast difference from my previous highly organised life with a system for everything to that of one where you made your own system and then had to make it work. My resettlement training period was spent with Racal-Chubb Security Systems Limited in West London where I found that a manger with just a desk, filing cabinet and telephone could run a major overseas contract quite efficiently without all the trappings I had to hand as a company commander in HM Forces.

At Chubb in Feltham I worked with Colin and Victor, my UK contacts, who would provide support throughout the project and, more importantly, ensure I got paid on time! I was introduced to Paddy Baker who would be the Contracts Manager with me on site. Paddy was a large ex-Irish Ranger who had served in Ghana during his time in the British Army and this suited everyone because he knew his way around. We prepared for the early days where it was planned that Paddy would travel first to Accra, set up our base and establish contact with our Dutch agent, and also to meet the Chief Executive and senior directors of the Volta River Authority. I remained in the UK preparing training aids, obtaining videos and writing lesson plans. How naïve I was, aiming for the moon when all that was needed was a handful of stars! Thanks go to a number of my friends at the Royal Military Police Training School who helped me out with a lot of basic training aids. I cannot reveal their names—no names, no pack drill! I thought I was ready for my project; I thought I knew what I was doing; I thought it would be just like another overseas exercise; as I said, all my contacts and, particularly Paddy, had been very economical with the truth. I was put a little at my ease when I visited the Ghanaian Embassy in London whilst collecting my visa; a more charming and helpful service you could not have wished for—so perhaps, I thought, this would be a sunshine tour after all!

At the end of the day there was always the amount of the year's salary to comfort me. I remember packing my suitcase and travel bag—how I had underestimated my needs I was soon to find out. Included in my medical box were anti-malaria tablets, anti-histamine pills, a TCP bottle, plasters, paracetamol tablets, suntan cream, water purification tablets and a self-inject anti-snake serum which may not be effective against some snakes! I also packed a Swiss army knife and another more robust double bladed knife for skinning or even killing. Foodstuffs included teabags, powdered milk, coffee jar, sweeteners and Marmite. Light clothing: short sleeve shirts, summer type trousers from Marks and Spencer (they did well with my large purchase), stout army officer type shoes, a lightweight rain smock, one tie, a lot of socks and underwear, and a spare pair of reading glasses from Boots to help with my paperwork duties; tissues for any orifice, and a small radio which was guaranteed to pick up the world broadcasts—they had never tried West Africa! The biggest mistake was not taking an electric kettle or bed linen, I suppose, but more of that later.

THE WAR YEARS

In the beginning of my life I won the lottery—I was born into a family from which I would receive love and affection and be able to enjoy the freedom of the countryside with all its wonders such as cows, cowshit, hops and trees that produced a variety of fruit.

I am told that my parents' marriage was an arranged matter between two wonderful grannies who brought together my Dad, Edward Thomas Bishop (Ted to all) and Nellie Irene Gittens (Nell). Dad was a confirmed bachelor farmer and Mum was a maid on some form of service in large houses in Kent. The stories she told me smacked of "Upstairs Downstairs" life as seen in the recent TV series. They married in January 1937. Dad, it is said, had sewn up the sleeve of his only suit with white thread, which was in evidence on the wedding day; Mum looked grand and carried Arum lilies. I came into the world at Lotland Farm on the road between Biddenden and Tenterden in Kent on the 6th September. Mum said that I had no eyebrows and this was due to being a little "premature" which in those days was most important, as the old village women would be wagging their tongues. At my christening I was named Roy Edward, but Granny Bishop wanted me to be Toby so, needless to say, that is how I became known. I still have two identities in Kent to this day: in Ashford I am Roy and in the villages I am Toby. Granny still rules.

Lotland Farm was 65 acres of Kent clay, nearly impossible to plough, and when it was turned it rolled over just like plasticine. Any crops that Dad tried were not a great success. We depended on an income from our ten dairy cows that produced two to three churns of milk per day for processing at the milk dairy at Headcorn. Without the monthly milk cheque we would have foundered earlier than we did. My brother Peter was born just over a year later and we started to grow up together. Life was hard on the farm with no electricity and our water supply came from a standpipe at the farm entrance some 600 yards away by the main road. Part of the daily routine was to refill our water churns for the house and to fill up to eight high-pressure lamps and hurricane lamps to illuminate the house at night. We had a fireplace in the main room with an inglenook big enough to take a huge duck's nest fire and a bench inset either side, if you could stand the heat. I remember using toasting forks that were almost a yard long so that you could toast without getting burnt. Life was basic, but I'm sure more enjoyable than living within a city with no fresh air and nowhere to scrump fruit or fish in small ponds with homemade rods.

The war came and I can remember our first air raid precautions with Dad digging an enormous hole at the side of the house that he lined with railway sleepers and then covered the roof with all the soil he had dug out. There was an igloo-type entrance and five people could just fit inside.

Living in "Hellfire Corner" as South East Kent was soon to be known was very dangerous, but for a young boy who did not really understand the total threat there was the exciting times that would fill my day. We collected the debris of war that fell onto our land, cannon shells, jettisoned items from fleeing or damaged aircraft, parachute silks and unfired or unexploded munitions which would have to be recovered by the Army or Home Guard or even the police. The skies above our farm roared with aircraft travelling in both directions and we soon became accustomed to the noise of those who were ours and those of the enemy. As was his want, my Dad went to the Man of Kent pub on a Saturday evening and sometimes he would take me along to sit in the landlord's rooms to enjoy a glass of lemonade and a packet of Smiths crisps with the blue salt packet in them. Whilst the patrons enjoyed their pint, the noise of opposing aircraft was ever present.

One Saturday, when things were very nerve-racking with the sounds of bombing in the Maidstone area, Dad said it was time to go and take refuge in the shelter. We left the pub with Dad carrying me up on his shoulders, as he was almost running to return to the farm. We were approaching the farm entrance when German aircraft started to bomb somewhat indiscriminately; perhaps they were unloading their bombs and running, or maybe they were trying for the railway line at the back of Lotland Farm. I heard the whistle of the falling bombs and Dad threw himself into the roadside ditch which was full of prickly brambles. Needless to say we were both badly scratched, and when we reached Mum shortly afterwards she thought we had been injured by the bombers! In those days medication for cuts and scrapes was the cow ointment that served all purposes and some iodine that hurt like hell when Mum patched up my scratches. Come the morning, we ventured out from our shelter and found bomb holes near the railway line some 800 yards away. We now made it routine to sleep in our shelter every night and I remember with fondness Dad searching for a large spider which had run across Mum's face and she would not go to sleep until it was killed.

By now we attended school despite the war restrictions. Air raid shelter drill was a regular occurrence and we were often confined to these bunkers. My brother and I used to sit in the fields watching young men kill each other and we used to cheer when a German went down and when it was one of ours we were glum. It was not unusual to come home and find Mum "entertaining" pilots or aircrew who had parachuted onto our fields. Brave young men of all nationalities briefly visited our farm where Mother's tea seemed to have a comforting effect. One Friday afternoon I met my first German officer. He was sitting in the kitchen looking pale and with a cut face. Dad was pressing a large pitchfork into his side and Mum was nattering about all and nothing, but I remember he shook so much he could not manage a cup and saucer so Mum poured his tea into my school mug. When the home guard arrived, he stood up, bowed to Mum and was gone.

I remember my second German pilot who looked exactly like all the pictures and drawings I had seen with black leather trousers and jacket and a white silk scarf. His left leg was broken and Dad was giving him a piece of his mind as some aircraft had strafed a herd of cows at Headcorn, killing most of them, and I think it if had not been for this man's injury Dad would have given him a sound beating. This German spoke perfect English and had the nerve to suggest he visit us when the war was won and he would be stationed in England. To my surprise my first American turned up to escort the German away; our local policeman was with them and I gathered that the Yanks would be now stationed nearby. The United States Air Force built a temporary aerodrome on the Halden Quarter lane not too far away which would be used for fighter aircraft in support of the invasion of France. The runways were made up of somerfield tracking, metal strips interlocked together and laid over a smoothed surface. The arrival of the Americans was well received and I know the landlord of the Man of Kent pub did well out of their custom.

It was at the Man of Kent that I saw my father lose his temper for the first time. A drunken young Yank was behaving badly towards the landlady despite having been cautioned by his comrades. When he found he was being ignored he made the mistake of turning on Dad and said he wanted to fight. Dad was quiet and I saw him start to bristle; when the stupid young man threw his drink over another lady present I heard Dad say, "Oh, all right then, me lad," and he pushed him out through the door into the garden, hit him once on the chin, picked him up completely and then threw him into the duck pen which was full of shit, rotten eggs and feathers. All this had been viewed by another American who had just arrived and shouted: "That's enough, airman!" The drunken airman by this time did not really know where he was as he could not find his way out of the mess he was in. The American officer's driver appeared and he and Dad got the drunk out to where there was a truck parked. He was placed in it and the driver stayed with him. The officer then offered to pay for any damages, bought Dad a drink and gave me his officer's tie in exchange for my school tie I was wearing. He said he would wear it when flying, as it would bring him luck. Sadly I never saw him again, but that brown air force tie stayed with me for a long time.

The war then in the main became dominated by the V1 Doodle Bug Rockets that crossed our farm heading for London. It was easy to identify them—rocket shaped with a high engine tail element and the sound a bit like a Volkswagen. Whilst you could hear the engine you knew you were okay, but when the engine cut out it was time to run for the shelter. They spiralled downwards and in the countryside it was the luck of the draw whether you got hit or not. They were not an accurate weapon. One of the worst incidents was where a flying bomb struck an orphanage near Sevenoaks, killing eight staff members and twenty-one children. It has been suggested it was targeted at Winston Churchill's house nearby.

One day early in the afternoon Peter and I stood mesmerised in our front field watching a V1 coming from our left when the engine cut out and it twisted down in the direction of the Man of Kent pub—but at the last second did a twist into a farmhouse behind Hukin's hop fields. There was a huge explosion and a black cloud of smoke rose into the sky. Dad set off running though it was about one and a half miles away.

This time there was a happy ending to this attack as the family in the farm had been watching the sky, like us, and had seen the lethal bomb turn towards them. They made a dash for the cider cellars under the barn and the V1 struck their house adjoining the barn. They emerged badly shaken, wet through with best Kentish apple cider, but alive! The hole left by that doodlebug eventually became a fishing pond containing the best roach and perch in the area. When Dad returned from helping out I noticed he was limping, and I asked him if he had hurt himself in the rescue. He said, "If you ran two bloody miles in your slippers, you would get sore feet too!"

My last bad memory of the war was a dreadful night-time incident when we heard the sound of a stuttering aircraft engine that was obviously a heavy bomber. We saw a flying fortress with a fire on board, circling the fighter drome with its crew clearly seen throwing items out of the doors. They were in desperate trouble and I thought it would attempt to land on the small fighter field. After two circles the fortress levelled out and I saw parachutes in the sky and then it turned towards the sea and disappeared. We never did find out the truth about the fate of that brave crew.

Finally, one could now feel that things were improving for us, for the arrival of prisoners of war on our farms confirmed that we were winning. The POWs worked well and all were glad to be out of danger. I do not know of any who abused their privileges and indeed many remained in the area after the war was over. There is one final little tale of the bomb shelter that became a super camp for the kids to play in. As youngsters do, they became interested in the birds and the bees, and one happy playing day we had friends on the farm and it just happened that Janet Smith and I were in the shelter playing doctors and nurses which somehow turned to a "if you show me yours, I'll show you mine" game. Whilst busy admiring each other's assets we were interrupted by my Mum who came to look for us as she had prepared tea. She caught us red handed or, shall I say, with no pants on! I received my first lecture of life and was sent to bed early—but not that early, as I heard Dad roaring with laughter when he was told the story.

I have a confession to make. Whilst visiting my Grandad and Grandmother Bishop at Halden Place Farm in Rolvenden on the Sussex border, I misbehaved! Halden Place was a large farm of dairy cows, hop fields and orchards, which kept Grandad more than busy. I must have had a mindless lapse on one visit when I took it upon myself to break every window in the dairy buildings. I cannot remember my punishment, but for those days I certainly deserved a thrashing. I wish I could now say sorry to my grandparents.

Granny Bish baked the finest apple pies and made the best butter around. I helped her in both ventures and that probably eased my conscience a little. Now that I'm a grandfather, I realise the important role one has in supporting one's grandchildren.

THE EARLY YEARS AFTER THE WAR

The worst happened—Dad and the farm were going under due to costs and the bad state of our economy at the time. We had to sell off the farm and its contents at auction. I remember it was a sad day when we had to say goodbye to the cows who we knew by name and had become pets in a way. The entire farm machinery was laid out in the main front field and the auction took place. We retained some bits of equipment including tools, a cart and hay rake and moved them and ourselves to Bush Farm which was down the lane by the Man of Kent pub out on the Halden Quarter and close to the American base. This smallholding was only 15 acres and again not suitable for good crop growing but would still be a kid's paradise playground with its trees, ponds and fields. There was no electricity but we did have a tap in the small kitchen. How my parents brought up three boys and two girls in this little old building I will never know. We were poor in cash but rich in family. Dad became a labourer on Podkin Farm, which was opposite, and somehow we got by. We supplemented our income by poaching rabbits and in season even picking the yellow primroses for resale in London by Mr Foster who had some sort of game shop there. We got 2/6p for a netted rabbit and 1/6p for a shot rabbit. We actually sold Mr Foster a pheasant that my brother Peter had found dead in the hedgerow that had died from some pesticide intake—we never dared ask if it went down well. Sorry, Mr Foster!

 The family now consisted of myself, brother Peter, sister Mary, brother Richard and sister Shirley. We sadly lost two brothers who died at childbirth in these difficult times. I was acutely aware at school that we were very poor as now I could compare things with my classmates. A school trip to Wenduine in Belgium was planned and I was the only outstanding person who had not paid their subscription. This embarrassment sticks with me to this day. Now, I am the one who has sufficient funds to do almost anything and my former school friends are still feeling the pinch in life. Thanks to a teacher called Mr Holden at Homewood Secondary School, I became a prefect and the House Captain of Sir William Hales House and this boosted my confidence. The Man of Kent pub continued to feature in our lives, and was still Dad's pub and the place where we parked our cycles every day to catch the bus to school.

It was around this time that I was introduced into the Methodist Church at High Halden. Firstly I attended Sunday School and then later in the normal Sunday services. I have in my house today the Methodist certificates outlining my success in various religious examinations. I did not realise just how important it would be to me to have joined this church. My Methodist service started with Sunday School once a week where my singing soon made me the leading member of the little choir. I suspect that my mother was responsible for us children joining the chapel. The minister was also the local shopkeeper and as we were members of his flock we received a sympathetic pricing on our groceries!

At 15 years old it was time for me to leave school, not having done too well, but I found that history and English were my strong subjects. The last week at school was when Dad announced, "There is a job for you up at the firm on Monday." He, by now, had entered the building trade and worked for W P Woodgate-Ltd in High Halden for better wages. I was told I was going to be a bricklayer apprentice but was too naïve to really take on board the full implications of this. My first pay packet was £1.3s.5p—a fortune for a 15 year old with 10s to mum for 'keep' and the rest mine! I still have that pay packet. My brother Peter was at Maidstone Technical College as his maths was better than mine. I attended the college for an oral test but flunked it on pure nerves—or was it because I did not know the answer? Peter at this time took the early decision to join the Army as a boy entrant and went off to The Boys Infantry Battalion at Plumer Barracks, Crownhill in Plymouth. I know he had a pretty hard time there but made it through to later join our county regiment, The Buffs, and he became a Buff for life. He was awarded the OBE for services to our country and has become a successful businessman following his retirement from H M Forces. Recently he was honoured by being appointed Deputy Lieutenant of Kent for his contribution to the county.

My start as a brickie went reasonably well. I could not say that I enjoyed it, but what else was there to do in our rural environment? There were the farms or some other unskilled job. The richest memory I have of my apprenticeship was the introduction of life by fellow tradesmen and my uncle Fred Bran who was a site foreman on Woodgates Ltd. Fred was a great favourite of mine; constantly humorous and outrageous, he made life for us all feel better. He served as a tank crewmember in the war and used to fascinate me with his soldier tales when he was in the mood. Fred also had a set of Army barbers hair cutting tools and he used to cut the hair of my brothers and I. This man was to have a great effect on me and I will be forever grateful for his advice and friendship. Rumour has it that Fred died in the ladies underwear department of Marks & Spencers—this certainly would have been his ambition!

My other friend, a fellow brickie, is Frank Bourne, one of a large family from High Halden and a kind, hard working honest man who took me under his wing. Frank served his National Service in the Middlesex Regiment most of the time in Korea as a bren gun carrier driver and experienced all the harsh times of that faraway war. He also recounted events when he was in the mood and I avidly listened to each word. It was from the friendship with these two ex-soldiers that gave birth to my becoming unsettled with laying bricks in all weathers and wondered perhaps if I would miss the chance to see something of the world they told of? Parallel to this, I had started courting a pretty girl in Tenterden, Margaret Broom, who's Dad managed the Mence Smith Ironmongers shop. I am not sure how we first met but I think we had been set up by our friends. Needless to say, our friendship blossomed, albeit I had my face slapped on one of our first meetings; but, amazingly, we are now still together after 45 years! How Maggie ever put up with me and the events you will read about one will never know. I am not too sure what Margaret's parents thought of me but they were kind enough not to say. I hope in the end I did not let them down.

I took the decision to break my apprenticeship and told Dad. He was not too happy but, bless him, he went along with me and indeed wrote his parental agreement letter for the firm. Most of my workmates were surprised and they thought I had gone mad. I detected a note of approval from Uncle Fred and Frank Bourne who probably would like to have returned to the Army. Why I chose the Royal Military Police I cannot remember, but now, looking back, it was the right choice and I know I did my Corps and the Army well. Chatham recruiting office saw me sign on and take my oath of allegiance and I was in. My Mum's mum, Granny Grace, had given me the train fare to get to Chatham and later on in life she would never take back the loan. On 20th August 1956 I commenced training at the Depot and Training Establishment RMP in Woking. Inkerman Barracks was an old female prison and had seen better days; the place was haunted: it was bleak and stuffed full of some 3000 regular and national servicemen undergoing training. 591 Squad under Sergeant George Waites was to be my place for 16 weeks of blurred shouting, continuous drill parades, weapons training, motor cycle training and classroom theory skills. After six weeks we were allowed out of barracks if you could pass the scrutiny of the regimental police staff who were not too fond of sprogs and delighted in bullying them about.

Talking about bullies, there was one squad that was always known as Beacon's Light Infantry. Beacon was a big man who moved his squad around at the double and to excess. To our delight one day he was giving his squad extra drill in the afternoon and was putting on a good show for the NAAFI girls who were sunning themselves in the late September warmth. He posed in his best twirls and shouted commands whilst grinning at the ladies. He brought his squad to the 'slow march', advancing towards the main building with himself stepping backwards to admire his work and also being able to let the girls see him. Alas, he stepped too far and disappeared down one of the main coal shoots on the face of the block! He emerged from the bowels of the building covered in coal to the applause of the NAAFT ladies and a squad with not a flicker of emotion on their faces. One awful rumour was spread throughout the barracks that he had the smallest penis in the permanent staff team despite being well over 6 feet tall. We were lucky in 591 squad. Sergeant Waites was firm but fair and we thanked our lucky stars he stayed with us until pass out in January 1957. My training period was over and I was a better person for it, despite having some boils, a motorcycle accident and losing a small piece of the small finger on my left hand—yes, I was the bloody idiot who let his finger go into the firing chamber of the sten gun, as well as being placed in close arrest for laughing on parade and having three haircuts in one day. I made it in spite of some doubtful forecasts from my instructors—I was still totally unaware that I would ever make a successful career in the Army.

My brother Richard, nine years younger than I, followed me into the Royal Military Police and enjoyed a full career. We had the privilege to serve together as is mentioned in this tale. He became a company commander and took his men to Iraq in Operation Desert Storm. He is well admired as a 'soldier's man' and he delights in following his rough shooting hobby with the help of his three Springer gun dogs. In my absence from the UK during my African trips I asked him to be proxy father for my children should I not return.

I am pleased to say this relationship remains, and happily there has been no need for his help!

Mention must also be made of my two sisters: Mary, born between Peter and Richard, and Shirley, the youngest. They both coped well with our often hard childhood and went on to marry successful and considerate partners who remain to this day enjoying rewarding marriages—my, how things have changed in just one generation to the troubled relationships we see now. I later found that during my travels somewhere in the world that my mother had carved out a reputation for herself as 'the walking grandmother'. She had participated annually in the international Nijmegen Marches in Holland, walking 25 kms per day for four days to gain the gold medal of achievement. Following that, she went on to support charitable causes in Kent by walking incredibly long distances. For most of the time I was unaware of her determined efforts but am now very proud because she was typical of our family. She was indeed a true 'Shropshire lass' who made a significant contribution to our country. The strength of our family bond forged by our beloved parents and grandparents has made us a formidable team and this has got us through to our now comfortable existence that is the envy of most.

THE BRITISH ARMY 1956–1986

A look into my Army service life with some incidents worthy of reading continues my path towards the time of the African decision. Sporting a single Lance Corporal's stripe on my arm on completion of training made me feel good, but I was soon to learn that my Corps was not the most popular body as we were the Army's policemen and had been given the nickname of 'redcaps' after the colour of our caps and a more derogatory name of 'monkeys' which had come from the last war when there was a popular music tune called *Little red monkey, monkey!* I made it my life's ambition to reverse any bad references to my Corps and put my heart and soul in learning the hard way the respect of all arms. I hope my contribution and that of many of my friends achieved that status.

The need for an officer to maintain good order and discipline in an army has been recognised in England for at least the last five hundred years. I quickly learnt that my Corps history stems from 1511 to current times where over the years the 'provost' supported the country's armies by maintaining discipline, and even carrying out punishments, which made them unpopular, and they became known as 'bloody provost'. It is from this source of mounted beginning that the Corps of Royal Military Police is derived.

1887 saw the formal inclusion of the Military Mounted Police (MMP) in the Army List and later followed by the Military Foot Police (MFP). Both served with great distinction in all the country's wars, reaching a peak of some 36,000 men and women in the Second World War. In 1946 King George VI granted the Corps the 'Royal' prefix. When I joined on the 20th August 1956 it was at the time of the Suez campaign and little did I know what the next 30 years would offer me. At the tender age of 19 years and not worldly wise, the future was unknown, but there was one thing for sure—there was no going back. The only way was forward, taking the rough with the smooth.

My first tour was with the 1st British Corps Provost Company stationed in Bielefeld, West Germany, in the same barracks that housed the home of the Headquarters 1st British Corps. The trip I remember from Woking to Bielefeld via Harwich and the Hook of Holland was a nightmare in the January 1957 bad weather. The flat-bottomed troopships rolled and bucked and I had seen some large amounts of spew coming out of grown men. I was lucky; I felt rough but was not sick and we were glad to reach Holland and get off those smelly vessels. The name of the worst vessel was the *Empire Parkeston*. I shall never forget this transporter of human misery. Then it was the troop train which called at every Garrison town in the British Army of the Rhine, dropping off the new drafts and picking up the time expired servicemen for their trip home. Bielefeld was just ten years after the end of the war and still showed signs of the devastation. The locals were friendly enough but there were many who did not like us. My unit enjoyed the doubtful nickname of '1st Brush Company' given to it by other RMP units as they seemed to think that all we did was sweep up leaves. The weeping willow tree in front of Block 8 Ripon Barracks has a lot to answer for. The six years I served in Bielefeld saw a meteoric rise in my career from Lance Corporal to Acting Sergeant; there was the lucky element, but that's how it goes. I bought a second-hand Volkswagen and was taught to drive by a chum and then had a British Forces Germany driving licence before I had a normal UK one; in those days you went home, showed your Army licence and had a full UK one issued.

My six years saw me start with duties as lowly as the one I mentioned, sweeping up leaves around Block 8, making sure that I was always busy when a senior rank passed by. I was classified as a 'DE', a direct entry as a regular soldier. The remainder and the majority of my comrades were national servicemen serving out their two years; they were not too keen on regular soldiers, but they accepted me and I made some firm friends from all over the UK.

The Regimental Sergeant Major (the RSM) was a wartime veteran called Abel. He was feared and we never passed his office unless it was absolutely necessary. I was summoned one day to see him and I wondered what my fate would be! He surprisingly was smiling and told me to relax as he had a project for me. He had designed a new rubbish area for the dustbins and waste materials and wanted it completed before the next visiting general's inspection. He had found that I had trained as a bricklayer and it was now my task to create his new venture. I was given the freedom from routine duties, and even a labourer to assist me, and I managed to make this project last for two weeks, enjoying every moment of my individual freedom. My chums gave me a hard time for being the blue-eyed boy but, as usual, good things don't last too long.

Two evenings each week I attended evening classes and taught myself to type and some other office skills and when a vacancy occurred in the main Corps Headquarters I found myself transferred into the Assistant Provost Marshals

(APM) office with two stripes on my arm! It was in 1959 that I took some leave and went home to Kent and married my teenage girlfriend, Margaret Broom. One of my fellow redcaps from the company, Roy Beale, also from Kent, acted as my best man. We had a fine wedding in Ashford and a short honeymoon in Brighton; such was the system in those days, and then it was back to Bielefeld where we took up residence in a one-room bedsit as a married couple. Our lodgings were the home of a German family who made feather duvets. Needless to say, we were always plagued by feathers. Living in one room was difficult. The small kitchenette could only take a Baby Belling Cooker with two cooking rings and a minute oven. The Christmas chicken had to be roasted first head end in and then turned around for the tail end! Toast was produced by laying the two-ring electric fire on its back. Happy days!

Eventually we moved into an army married quarter and life became more comfortable. There we would stay until 1962 when a posting order arrived for our next tour in Singapore. Three stripes now graced my arm and we were financially sound to meet the challenge of this major move. Before we left Bielefeld and 1st British Corps Provost Company RMP in 1962, I had the opportunity to see the end of the National Service conscription requirement for the United Kingdom. This was history in the making. There was no longer the requirement to pressgang young men into the service of their country. There had been some under estimation for the continued manning of The British Army of the Rhine and thousands of young national servicemen had their two-year contract extended by six months. This caused an enormous morale problem for a short time but in typical British fashion our 'nashes' as we called them settled down and served out their time. Our country should be eternally grateful to them. These men undoubtedly qualified for the award of The National Service Medal that now exists on a self-claim basis. Also at this time I made a major error. My father-in-law informed me that there were a pair of terraced cottages for sale in Ashford and he thought we should buy them as an investment. I did not listen and that proved to be a bad mistake. I could have had them for £750 each and when we returned from the Far East they were worth £5000 each. Such is life.

The trip to that Far Eastern military outpost was made in a prop-driven Britannia aircraft and was long and tedious. We flew out of Stanstead, first to Turkey (5 hours), then on to Bombay (9 hours) and finally to Singapore (10 hours). Both airports at start and finish were not much more than large tin hangers. The heat of Singapore hit us as we came off the aircraft and stayed with us until we left. There was not a great deal of activity until the Borneo war of confrontation with Indonesia where President Soekarno tried to grab Brunei, Sabah, Borneo and others for himself. He did not achieve his aim and it cost him dearly. Margaret decided to return to the UK and the heat was getting her down and I finished off my time there which would bring me up to my 9-year termination day. I flew home wondering what the hell I was going to do as the soldiering I had been exposed to so far and the jobs I had been given were mundane and soul destroying which led to an excessive consumption of the amber liquid and the turbulence that goes with it. I was not the best soldier that Britain demanded.

At home we had a few days to consider life and it became apparent that the Army still offered the best opportunities that were available. I drove to the RMPTC (Royal Military Police Training Centre) now based in the home of the Royal Sussex Depot, Rousillon Barracks in Chichester. I had also been pleased to hear that my brother Richard had followed me into the Corps and was now serving in Verden in North Germany. I walked into the postings office in Chichester and said, "I'm back—please post me to somewhere where I can do some real work." I noticed that a sergeant winked at the civilian clerk and said, "We do have a vacancy for a senior corporal in 4th Guards Brigade Provost Unit in Iserlohn. You'll have to sacrifice your third stripe—is that OK?" It took me two seconds to respond. "Yes, that will do," I said, not knowing it was going to be the best decision I could ever have made in my life!

4th Guards Brigade was located in Aldershot Barracks, Iserlohn, and just down the road was Mons Barracks currently housing a Scottish battalion and a little further away in Menden, 50 Missile Regiment was based. Within a short time of arriving at the brigade unit and, met by WO 2 (Stick) Tonkiss and Staff Sergeant Lambert, I realised that I was in a different world and my gut feeling was that I would enjoy it. The Officer Commanding Captain Brian Rawlings was a large fit man who had such leadership skills that his men would run over a cliff for him. He was a parachute-trained officer and had recently completed a tour with The Sultan of Oman's forces. The unit members were much fitter than I and on our first run over the hills I almost blew a gasket trying to keep up with my comrades. This comradeship was the finest I had experienced and it was noticeable that all areas of the UK were represented there: Taffys, Jocks, Paddys, Scousers, Brummies and even Men of Kent. This mix was the best cocktail ever seen and we proved it by being the best provost unit in the Corps area. To cap what was my finest posting was the arrival of my son Martin. Margaret and I were considering buying a Mercedes now that we could afford it, but I was happier with my son and to this day he is known as 'our Merc'.

Amongst the many and varied operations we undertook was those of border patrols on the inner East/West German border in the Hannover region. Some six vehicles each containing two RMP and led by a lead vehicle from the British Frontier Service would patrol along a given stretch of the wire showing the flag and reporting incidents and intelligence sightings. Patrols were only conducted in daylight and each evening of the weekly patrol we would base ourselves at a farmhouse or in village halls wherever we could find accommodation. During the third day out we suddenly came upon an East German working party repairing the fence a few yards from us. I saw that a red tape had been laid on the ground in front of them and between us. I enquired from the BFS man what it was for and he said it was the death line for anyone from the DDR party should they make a dash for freedom. We then decided not to encourage anyone to try on this occasion. The DDR soldiers photographed us photographing them, no words were exchanged and we moved on. My brother Richard had joined my unit as I had used an old army system whereby a brother could claim a brother; again, for both of us, this was the best thing that could have happened and we went on to complete parallel successful careers.

Richard was on a patrol with me and when we stopped for the night we sorted ourselves out and a guard was posted. The rest of us were given free time to enjoy a drink at the local *gasthof*. All went well until the burly landlord tried to take a swing at our cook who was only a little lad. Don McNiven then had to sort out the landlord! We all staggered back to the barn where our sleeping bags were laid out. We crashed out and the barn was filled with farts and snores. Sometime during the night I woke to hear Richard calling, "Brother, where are you—I'm stuck!" I went outside into the moonlight and there he was in the chicken pen, having gone for a pee and somehow entering the pen instead of the barn door. He had chicken shit up to his knees and was trying to find his way out. We got him back inside the barn and he had a very early morning wash at the water point. These patrols proved popular and took us away from normal garrison duties and the routine. From this tour in my life I still now maintain contact with those friends made in this special family. It is also worthy of note that on a percentage basis this unit produced more officers commissioned from the ranks than any other. Thanks to Colonel Brian Rawlings a few good men found their way in life and he is owed a great deal.

Camp du Larzac—where the bloody hell is that? We were soon to find out. Elements of the Fourth Guards Brigade were to exercise in Southern France for six months and there was a requirement for a detachment of Royal Military Police to accompany them. It was midsummer when the road party set off from Germany. A lot of the vehicles were ten-tonners, which meant it would be a slow process in reaching our destination.

Larzac is a plateau on top of the Massive Central area above the town of Millau and some one hundred kilometres from the Mediterranean. Armies have trained at Larzac for hundreds of years and the little stone village of La Cavalerie only comes to life when there are resident military forces.

The camp has been used as a prisoner of war facility for both French and German armies. There is little on the plateau except for grazing animals—the two roads at either end are narrow and winding and very dangerous; one could see the evidence of smashed and broken vehicles as one peered down into the ravines. After four days travelling the Brits had arrived. Two little cafes and a shop had opened following their arrival. The townsfolk of Millau at the foot of the mountain were not too friendly; they were part of Vichy French who supported the Nazis during the Second World War and did not welcome us with open arms—they were happy providing we stayed on the plateau.

A fond memory of Camp du Larcaz was my being awoken early one morning. The dawn was breaking and I thought I could hear a radio playing somewhere. I was wrong—it was singing. Eventually the singers arrived. A battalion of the French Foreign Legion was moving in to exercise with us and they had marched from Millau station to Larzac. Their discipline was perfect: they actually looked as if they were enjoying themselves. We were to make good friends amongst their ranks. I met an Englishman from Sussex who was completing his five-year engagement, and he was considering extending his time.

All their officers were French, the majority of the sergeant majors were German and the main group seemed to come from Eastern Europe. Meal times were something to look forward to. Red wine was served with every meal plus litre bottles of non-alcoholic beer, which were still standing in their crates in the British area the day they left!

We exercised backwards and forwards; the red sandy soil of Larzac covered all and everything—even the canopies of the vehicles turned reddish brown. Then came the bad news for me. My brother Peter was serving as an instructor with officer cadets at Sandhurst and had been involved in a traffic accident at Vogelsang Training Area in southern Germany and was very seriously injured. He had been transferred to the British Military Hospital in Iserlohn, the home of 4th Guards Brigade, and where I had my married quarter. I was collected from Camp du Larzac by Captain Brian Rawlings on his flying visit and we drove like fury back to Germany and Iserlohn. My brother had sustained a major head and face wound, having been "rolled on" by the Landrover he had been travelling in. After many operations and suffering great pain he was patched up and brought back to military fitness to continue soldiering on. He was a lucky man.

One funny occurrence from Larzac was that on rare occasions we were taken to the sea at Cap d' Adge, South of Montpellier, to rest and take the sea air. This was a popular outing as the beaches were full of beautiful girls. The Army organiser made a mistake by placing the military party alongside a nudist colony. As the time neared for them to gather and return to base, the officer in charge noticed that 70% of the men were missing! The sergeant major informed him that the men were in the nudist colony and were happily viewing the seaside! The officer tried to enter the nudist area but was turned away by the burly security guards. After some discussions he stripped off down to just his socks and brown shoes, rammed his officer's cap on his head and strode into the camp calling for his dog Rufus to follow him. He made for the large group of white-bottomed soldiers conducting their bird watching hobby near a group of young ladies and managed to round them up and return to the pickup point. By the time the soldiers had reached Larzac and consumed several crates of beer en route they were singing 'for he's a jolly good fellow' in appreciation of their officer's actions; the sergeant major was just praying that his camera had taken some reasonable pictures for the Sergeant's Mess!

All good things came quickly to an end and it was off to the Junior Tradesmen's Regiment in Rhyl, North Wales. I became a Platoon Sergeant in Cassino Platoon, JTR Rhyl. I was responsible for some 45 young guys who joined at 15 years and would eventually go on to join the main adult army in various trades. I have nothing but admiration for the junior tradesmen—still children but expected to do a man's lot. I know of many who went on to become the senior ranks, warrant officers and officers in their corps.

A funny story from the JTR Rhyl times—everyone had to have a hobby that was intended to fill the spare time for the youngsters and take up the spare time of the permanent staff. Mine was the sailing hobby and we spent most of our time repairing an old fibreglass GP 14 foot sailing dinghy in a hanger although we never did much sailing and I actually do not like sailing and the sea. Sergeant Field, a Platoon Sergeant, ran the fencing hobby; he was a cocky individual, God's gift to women, as you know. He received an invitation to teach one evening per week at the girls' boarding school opposite the camp gates and for two weeks we put up with his stories of pulling the girls, how wonderful they thought he was and there was a good chance that the gym mistress would bed him soon. Returning from an evening driver training session with one of my platoon, I saw a cluster of people outside the medical centre door and went over to see what was going on. To my joy there was Sergeant Field with one of his fencing foils protruding from his upper arm. He was right about the gym mistress—she got him all right, right in his courting arm! He never said a word again but all over the camp guys were seen to be shadow fencing when he was around.

Kinmel Park Camp at Rhyl was soon behind me and, now holding the rank of Staff Sergeant, I was off to West Bromwich to help run 116 Provost Company TAVR and their Senior Permanent Staff Instructor. I tried to return to a normal general duty unit but my records office insisted that this was in my career planning and now later I can say they were exactly right. West Bromwich was a friendly place; the TA Centre was in Carters Green at the end of the High Street. The TA buildings were old but functional and housed all the company's vehicles and stores. We had detachments at Manchester and Cardiff which I visited on a regular basis and the company would come together for our annual camp and training weekends. The Officers and men making up the TA Company were the opposite from my last posting. These guys were mature no-nonsense individuals who were very professional. Our role was to support the 1st British Corps in BAOR and bi-annually we did our camp normally in the Sennelager area. I still meet some of my old comrades from the Midlands annually at our Corps gathering at Westminster Cathedral on the remembrance weekend and Jim Ramsey in particular who never misses this parade—sorry, Jim, I forget your BEM! My experience with the TA improved my administrative skills and my man management. Crikey, I'd done them all now—juniors, TA, mature men and you name them. My fondest memory of the TA Centre was that the daffodils in the garden of a small rabbit hutch Victorian house had soot on them from the industrial fallout. Someone recently told me that my old white VW was still there which I bought whilst in the Guards Brigade.

Our worst memory of West Bromwich is when we lost our little son Martin who had wandered out of the Centre compound through a wicket gate that had not locked properly. My wife and I ran around in circles as soon as we found him missing. We enlisted the aid of two unit members and then left the centre to look in the nearest streets. As I went down the High Street towards Birmingham, there, some distance away, was our little boy returning towards me and holding the hand of the biggest black Rastafarian I had ever seen! That kindly man had found him wandering on the pavement and Martin had told him that his house was with the 'soldiers'. We owe a great debt to our rasta man.

Before my leaving West Bromwich I was yet again promoted to Warrant Officer, Class 2, a CSM. This confirmed that my records office had got me on the right career path. Captain Peter Brock, my Permanent Staff Officer at the unit, asked, "Do I have to call you mister now?" I bought myself a stupid hat because it was the done thing but it didn't suit me. The unit establishment table did not allow for a warrant officer on its strength so I was on the move again, this time to Edinburgh and the 170 Provost Company RMP based in the castle itself. Many of my friends in the Corps were Scottish so I was more than interested to see their homeland. It was not too long, a journey from Birmingham to Waverley Station in Edinburgh. I arrived at 5:30 a.m. and there was my welcoming party to drive up to the castle. My first impression was that it was a grey city, a reflection from the granite buildings that surrounded me. It was odd to be standing on top of our castle looking around the city and across into Fife. My welcome breakfast meal included a wee dram of whisky, which at that time of the morning seemed out of order, but as I learnt, when in Rome do as the Romans do. I think that wee dram was the start of my liking for that amber liquid which remains my favourite tipple. It was a great posting, with the Edinburgh Military Tattoo, the one o' clock gun ceremony, beating retreat and all the pomp and colour connected with the castle's tourist activity. We enjoyed physical training in the hills around Cornrie at Cultybraggan Training Camp. Here I saw my first salmon making its way inland to its spawning grounds. The sight of these magnificent fish was a sight to behold. I took on board more of Scotland's history than I can now remember. It was a great privilege being the English Sergeant Major of a jock unit.

Martin started school in Longstone and it was not long before he started to say 'aye' instead of 'yes'. To all those who joke about the Scots being mean and tight with their money, I say try a visit yourself and enjoy the hospitality which was extended. Just like Welsh Army units with everyone called Jones, we had the same experience with McCleod. I can still remember the last three numbers of McCleod 577 and McCleod 337 from the Isle of Lewes. This posting was only marred by the shooting of Jimmie Nylan, a young corporal who constantly pestered me for a posting to Northern Ireland. I let him go and to my anger found that the IRA had shot him in the back twice whilst he was on an unarmed foot patrol in Belfast. He survived but is partially crippled. If I could turn the clock back I would. Jimmie, if you read this, I salute you.

My finest performance in Edinburgh came after Margaret and I attended a Robbie Burns supper high in the old medical block which features in all the tourist photographs. The haggis was fine, the pipe music fascinating and the whisky flowed, of course. The speeches were confusing as people addressed the haggis; this, the ladies and the ceremonial stabbing of that much-lauded dish really made our night. I cannot remember a great deal of the journey home, but sufficient to say I was feeling quite well and I do remember Margaret saying something about having stopped taking the pill—but too late! To our joy nine months later we were blessed with the arrival of Victoria. Thank God for Robbie Burns! Indeed, we now make a special effort to commemorate his birthday every year. In fact, we rather like haggis. I named my daughter Victoria as a mark of respect for my old commanding officer, Brian Rawlings, whose leadership had such a pronounced effect upon my life. We remain closely in touch to this day. His daughter, Victoria, shares the same habits, individuality, stubbornness and beauty and God help the man who upsets them!

After Edinburgh it was off to 247 (Berlin) Provost Company. On arrival in Berlin I was met by Sergeant Jock (Robbie) Robertson who had been part of the Guards Brigade family. We drank too many Schulteis Beers on that first evening and I felt terrible when standing before Major David Eking on my initial interview, but thank God he was obviously well briefed and invited me to sit down and have a cup of coffee. "You are off to Helmstedt Checkpoint," he said, "Major Colin Watkins is downstairs and will drive you down the autobahn corridor in his car." Major Colin Watkins was a charming man and a good shot. Helmstedt was where East met West on the Inner German Border. On top of our autobahn control duties at the checkpoint for travellers to the Allied Sector of Berlin we managed to train by shooting regularly against the German Police and their MPs, the Feldjaeger, and being beaten by them in every football game we played. Life was fairly pleasant.

The Helmstedt Russian character I will never forget was Major Gonchorov of the Soviet Army who was an animal. Major Gonchorov used to stand at the Soviet checkpoint buildings ogling the western travellers and making obscene gestures. He admired the modern cars that did not exist in the East. He was a beast of the field, interested only in pornography, eating and shouting at his juniors. I know regular supplies of porn books were handed over to him as he met people in no-man's land, exchange salutes, pretend to shake hands and then stuff his magazines down the front of his trousers; they never fell out because of the size of his huge legs and the high Russian boots he wore. I would imagine him at the front of a charge by Russian soldiers; it would take a tank to stop him. I used to exchange daily chitchat with him and give him a decent UK newspaper and in return he gave me *Pravda*, not very interesting reading about the total strawberry crop in the Ukraine or the latest tractor production figures. I saw the weakness of the Soviet Army system there: everyone was incapable of acting as an individual and orders had to come from a superior rank. One example was when an automatic barrier failed at the checkpoint on the Soviet side: the young soldier was left helpless, he gathered up all the western travellers that were stationary and marched them for 2kms to the main office, leaving their cars locked at the side of the roadway. He received some orders and then marched his fuming guests all the way back to their cars before waving them through. Any soldier who entered a room where an officer was present had to stop, salute and ask permission to pass. The young conscripts were housed badly, fed badly and paid badly. I saw the delivery of the bread one day. Square dark loaves thrown into the back of an open lorry. It was raining heavily and I wondered what it would be like when it was time for consumption. They had two uniforms—one for summer and one for winter, and they stank. I now know that the old German soldiers were right, that if you were downwind of a Soviet unit you could smell them.

My promotion to Regimental Sergeant Major (Warrant Officer Class 1) came whilst I was at the Helmstedt Border Crossing Checkpoint. It was something I had only dreamt of and it took some time for the fact to sink in that I was going to be one of those very important and sometimes unpopular people who made a unit function in whichever way they wanted. I elected to be a humane individual and my own sometimes bitter experience had qualified me to know how to lead and supervise in the new style army where there was now not the large numbers of the 50s and 60s. In celebration of this promotion and new posting the young men and women of the Helmstedt unit dined me out at a country restaurant up against the inner German Border within sight of the Eastern DDR land. Following the meal, we adjourned to the only nightclub in Helmstedt to continue the festivities. We were able to walk back to our beds and on the way we played silly games like leapfrogging over the street fire hydrants. My foolishness led me to catch my suit jacket on top of one, causing me to take a header onto the pavement! My forehead bears signs of the embarrassing scars from this bump still today. My posting as RSM of 101 (Army) Provost Company RMP in Dusseldorf arrived and off I went in my ageing Fiat 124 to the Flughafen Kaserne (Airport Barracks) located alongside the civil main airport for Dusseldorf. The barracks were old and the maintenance of the buildings was a challenge in itself. The duties were not too arduous and I found that I could cope with the administrative demands and the operational requirements.

The tale from Dusseldorf must be the one where I inadvertently injured myself with a label staple. Whilst changing my uniform in the Sergeant's Mess, I picked up a freshly dry-cleaned pair of the green barrack dress trousers and jumped into them as I was in a hurry. I experienced a needle-like prick to my testicles, which made me jump. I was not prepared for the bleeding that followed. I panicked a bit as I could not stop it and was faced with having to go to the medical centre with a roller towel wrapped around my balls whilst sitting in the car. Worse followed. The duty staff nurse was Mrs Sue Lynes, wife of Corporal John

Lynes, one of my NCOs. There I was, lying on the examination bed with my best bits exposed to those who wanted to see if a Regimental Sergeant Major had any balls or not. To say I was embarrassed was to put it mildly; a nurse with her finger on the offending wound and her colleague spraying the area with plastic skin to stop the bleeding. I could not believe that so much blood could come from so small a wound and indeed from averagely small parts. The bleeding stopped and I got dressed and then considered how I could face the world when the tale of the testicles got around. I waited for the first unit comic to circulate a joke or two but surprisingly there was none and if there was it was done without my knowledge. The moral of this story is check that you take off the dry-cleaning label and remove the metal staples before donning your clothes.

The time at Dusseldorf passed fairly quickly. My family were with me, my brother and his wife were part of my unit and generally times were good. This was not to last and along came the posting order that was long overdue for me—Northern Ireland, where most of my colleagues had already served and it was time for me to do my bit for this troubled land.

Although I knew a great deal about Northern Ireland, particularly from talking to my colleagues who had served there since 1969, I never really understood the mindless violence and tribal hatred generated by the republican areas and the loyalist areas. I was given the appointment of WO 1 Int in the intelligence platoon of the 2nd Regiment Royal Military Police operating in East Belfast and the Twinbrook enclave near Anderson Town. Can you imagine it, there were actually two regiments consisting of military policemen, almost unheard of. 1st Regiment RMP was based at Aldergrove near the airport. We each had our own areas of responsibility (TAORs) and we worked alongside all the units of the British Army as they rotated through their six-month emergency tours; we for some reason had to do a straight two-year tour. Our duties were dangerous and like other units took our own casualties and scored successes against the terrorists of all factions. I remember one night lying on the roadside behind a bridge parapet near Mountpottinger having been fired on by Protestants at 11 p.m. and then later at midnight by the IRA. I thought what the bloody hell is going on, who the hell are we protecting and why not let them shoot it out themselves; but it was not as easy as that as time shows. I saw buses in the sky having been blown up and scenes of horror that remain with me still to this day. The sight of the gasworks explosion near the city centre where one of three gasometers was blown into the night sky looked just like the mushroom cloud explosion of a nuclear bomb. We took comfort that on this occasion the IRA had scored an own goal by killing themselves as they primed their bomb at the perimeter fence; come daylight, the seagulls showed us where their remains were lying. So it went on.

The IRA killed some of us and we killed some of them. It was a war without end and the cost in lives was unforgivable. It was odd to see foot patrols of a dozen military policemen making their way carefully through the narrow terraced streets. We knew most of the baddies by name as we were there for two years at a time. I was not happy going on patrol to update my knowledge dressed as a WO 1 so I borrowed the cook's beret and his self-loading rifle (SLR) which I favoured; it was heavy but had the power to stop an elephant. Not all was bad; my family actually joined me in NI and we had a quarter at Lisburn where sort-of normal life existed. My son attended the local school there and my thanks go to the Headmaster and his staff who rebuilt his education after some three other schools where the broken learning had done him no good. I was impressed with the old fashioned discipline and the high standards achieved. It seemed sad that in such a highly qualified land for both communities that learning could not overcome hatred and lead to peace.

Now came another bombshell for me—I had been selected for a commission in the Corps and suddenly a new world was open to me.

I was surprised and a bit apprehensive about my new opportunity. I was more of a doing person rather than a decider and planner. Would I be able to fit in with the new environment offered to me? Then I thought of all the officers I had known in the Corps and outside and decided that, bloody hell, if they could do it, so could I.

My wife at this point decided to buy a house in Ashford near to her parents' shop. Sadly we had lost her Mum but her Dad I know was absolutely chuffed that I had made it in my life. I had not let them down and this was important to me.

Margaret had followed the bugle for nearly twenty years and that was a good innings and also the children's education was now paramount for them. When I received my officer's uniform allowance, off I went to a respectable gentleman's outfitters in Bond Street and bought the accessories that any normal officer would need, albeit I thought it a bit old fashioned. There were spurs, of all things, to be worn with the Corps Mess kit; originally we were a mounted organisation, hence the spurs. Officer's small stick, pips, badges, hats, etc., followed, and soon I was almost there. I received my confirmation of commissioning and a posting order to 160 Provost Company, RMP in Aldershot, where I would hold the appointment of Operations Officer. My main role was to run the operational field force element in support of 6 Field Force who were the rapid reaction force of the UK and made up almost entirely of parachute units. The RMP parachute element had disbanded some time before and although it had now been reformed my field force element on my arrival was somewhat of an in-between group of some trained parachutists and some as myself feeling a bit out of the airborne family and known to the paras as 'crap hats'.

I was apprehensive as I made my way to Aldershot, newly commissioned and facing a number of challenges. The grapevine had informed me that the RSM at 160 Pro Coy RMP, a failed contender for a commission, had announced that he would not work with whoever took my appointment. I found him to be the worst bully and ignorant warrant officer not deserving of his rank. Further, I had to enter and live in a parachute mess full of gung-ho young officers and there I was, a 40-year-old 'crap hat' with nothing in common that could form a basis for my entry into their team. A young intelligence officer, Mike Charters, took me under his wing and met me at the mess door and my new world opened up for me. The Force Commander, Brigadier Mike Gray, welcomed me to his force and we found that we were on the same wavelength. I respected him and gave my best. As I was leaving his office he said, "By the way, Roy, will you go down to Depot Para and jump out of an aeroplane? There's a good chap." Bloody hell, I thought, what have I done?

Somewhat nervously, I visited Depot Para and the staff said I could volunteer for a water jump into the sea at Studland Bay near Poole Harbour. I was listed as a 'non jumper' and earmarked for ground training at the Pitts Road Training School close to my office. I was taught basic skills which included jumping off a high ledge and where your drop was arrested by a large fan just before you hit the floor. Following the fan experience we were taught to release ourselves from the parachute harness, as we would be descending towards the sea. Some time passed and then came the brown envelope—report to Depot Para at 06:00 hours and be coached to RAF Odiam to meet the RAF C130 transport aircraft and its crew who would be delivering us to our drop site. There were seven 'non-jumpers' like myself and I noticed that we were the quietest on that coach ride—I wonder why.

At Odiarn we debussed at a large hanger and signed a document that released the Army from any obligations should I be killed or injured, as I was a volunteer. We were then issued our parachutes from the back of a stores truck that had arrived and to my concern I noticed mine was labelled 'time expired'. I immediately felt the need to visit the toilet. Fortunately one of the other guys had noticed his was also labelled and enquired from the truck driver if they were all right. We were assured that this was the last jump for these chutes and it would not be helped in any way by their immersion in seawater; one felt just a little bit easier on learning this. We then donned our parachutes, making sure the harness was secured as taught; then we were checked over by the RAF Sergeant Dispatcher who said, "Don't worry gentlemen, I'll keep an eye on you and help you along." I was soon to find out what he really meant. We were then marched in single file out to where the C130 was parked and we emplaned in allocated sticks of 5. I found I was in the second stick and also second man in the stick. I found that adjutant of 1 Para was the first man and behind me was Dick Gittens, another officer, and I'm sure the plot was to ensure that I went where I was supposed to go. One of my chums who was in a later stick said that he had been giving me the thumbs up as I stood waiting hooked on for the approach to the door but I saw nothing as I was busy convincing my brain that I knew it was illogical to jump out of a perfectly serviceable aircraft and that I had not forgotten how to swim! We had a deflated life jacket under the harness and we were told to inflate it a little by a few puffs and that we could totally inflate it when we were in the water if we needed to.

It was time—we shuffled forward to the door and suddenly we were on our way. I remember the dispatcher holding my shoulder and then I was out riding down the slipstream and not knowing whether I was on my arse or my elbow. The chute opened and it drew my head up and there it was, a beautiful T10 canopy, no twists; I had two seconds or so to see the Hercules circling for its next run and then I saw yachts and boats from a seagull's view. My problem was how to judge the distance I was from the sea's surface? Normally one can gauge height because the eye has trees and houses to compare with but there was nothing near to us that the eye could take a bearing on. I went into my getting out of the harness drill, strike the release box then undo the leg straps and I hung in the harness on the strength of my arms. When I thought it was the right moment I let go of the harness, throwing it to the back of me and put my feet together to enter the water. I was lucky the chute drifted away from me and I went into the sea from about six feet; it was dark and I had water up my nose, but I bobbed back to the surface and I felt like Popeye the sailor full of spinach.

I swam to the Royal Marines rescue boat and they pulled me on board. The Royal Marine rescue boats were busy dashing over the sea's surface picking up sea jumpers. There was one non-jumper who got out of his harness far too early and I heard him squeal all the way down to the water, but he made it. From the rescue boats we were placed on board a larger sea-going launch and were welcomed by the CO of Para 1 who had been the drift man who jumped from the aircraft before all of us. All 63 men who jumped made it safely and the time-expired chutes had done a good job. We docked at Poole Harbour and there was our coach to take us back to Aldershot. I fell asleep on the coach and when I woke near our destination I found a brand new parachute jump smock on my lap. I never did find out who donated this gift, but I knew I was now fairly 'respected' in the eyes of my parachute colleagues. This was an experience that I would never forget and never regret. My greatest pleasure was also finding that the bully of an RSM in my unit had chickened out on an invitation to jump that day and had given his place to a young sergeant who followed me out in the fifth stick. Noise and power by appointment does not necessarily produce guts!

Shortly afterwards we were warned for exercise in North Germany and the Danish border and then onto Italy for a NATO support exercise on the Yugoslav border near Udine. The North Germany training went well but wet; we almost developed webbed feet, the field force regrouped north of Hohne with some elements going home after rest and recuperation in the fleshpots of Hamburg and the parachute element entrained for Pordenone in North East Italy. The train journey was bloody awful, cramped, water ran out in the toilets and the three-day trip was a test of one's patience; but we eventually staggered out onto a little station platform surrounded by curious Italians. We billeted with the local 5th Infantry Division whose role it was to protect the area facing Yugoslavia; the solders were mostly young national servicemen whose lot in the army was not a happy one. When I saw the barrack defences I asked my Italian contact if the walls and wire systems would be useful if attacked, and he said it was to keep the soldiers *in*!

The main parachute force from 1 Para jumped onto a zone nearby and we exercised with the Italians culminating in a major firepower demonstration, including the use of battle tanks and supporting ground attack aircraft. The local people did not like soldiers of any form and we were not received well; in one newspaper I saw the headlines "The barbarians have landed" which smacked a little of their history. The exercise terminated and we began to regroup in various barracks around Pordenone. I was in the village of Istrago with a group of Italians when suddenly there was a massive explosion off to our right where what looked like a small nuclear mushroom burst followed by houses, cars and trees all going skywards. The Italians were rooted to the spot and as the blast came at us I had to push them down to try and take cover; but they just wanted to look, not knowing the impact danger. The last was slightly diverted by a mound nearby and we only sustained minor cuts and bruises from flying objects. There was total confusion and the Italians were milling around and shouting.

I spoke to Sergeant Allen, my section commander, who was nearest the epicentre of the explosion and had a vehicle and radio that was working. He took an

Italian Colonel with him who was not too keen but they made their way into the devastation hampered by overhead power cables that were lashing about sending sparks everywhere, and the mostly deadly problem was found to be red hot hissing 105mm tank shells spread over the ground. It was found that there was a military munitions factory alongside a commercial firework factory and on occasions there was an exchange of explosive materials. On this occasion a fire had started in the firework factory, causing a small explosion leading to the munitions factory being totally destroyed and thus the scattering of munitions over a wide area. The locals went berserk, blaming it all on the fire power demonstration that day and they even stoned us as we were trying to help in the aftermath; even priests were shaking their fists. Eventually the cost was found to be that 25 civilians were missing, 'totally dispersed' in the words of one newspaper. Some soldiers taking a shower after their exercise had glass fragments in their arses, but the Brits came off light.

Sergeant Allen and his team behaved in a manner expected of our soldiers and they eventually received commendations from the General Officer Commanding South East District on return to Aldershot. I was proud of my RMP element. Life in the 6th Field Force was good for me and I felt at home. A trip to Gibraltar followed where, with a small team of five NCOs I was given the task of training 30 Gibraltar Services Policemen employed by the Ministry of Defence in anticipation of the reopening of the border with Spain which had been closed for a long time. It was felt that extra security would be needed for the RAF Station and the Naval Dockyards. This was a fairly nice tour with lovely sunshine and a regular training programme. Our students were bright young officers and keen to learn. Whilst we were in 'Gib' we did the usual things like the rock tour, the apes and the caves, some fishing off the point and even a trip over to Tangiers. Soon, alas, it was time to get back to reality and it was home to sunny Aldershot and back to military training. My family had the opportunity to visit for a three-week break from the UK and my son Martin caught a sea bream on corned beef!

"Good morning, Roy," said the Field Force Commander, "How is life?" I assured Brigadier Gray that all was well and that I was having a useful and rewarding time as his policeman. He smiled and informed me that there was to be an exchange of officers from his force and members of the Germany Army and that I would be going to Hannover to spend three weeks with the Feidjager Dienst Kommando, the new model of their military police, far from the old dreaded 'head hunters' of the second world war. I was to be housed in the German Army Officers School in Hannover and join in their training and visit operational units around Northern Germany.

I was made most welcome by my German counterparts; everyone wanted to talk to the single Brit in the college and their conversation was all based on war. The morning assembly was an odd experience. We paraded in a three-sided square, five ranks deep, facing the saluting dais on which the school commandant greeted us and took the salute of the student officers. One morning we stood in our massed ranks waiting to receive the commandant's 'thought for the day'. He puffed out his chest and shouted, "My thought for today is—kill tanks!" "Yawohl Herr Oberst!" came the reply, "Kill tanks!" The band struck up a rousing marching-tune and off we went around the parade ground with flags flying, music blaring and the young officers singing. I suddenly felt that I understood how easy it would be to motivate these fine young men into military machines.

My time with these well-motivated and hospitable men had come to an end. I was invited to a small drinks party in the club opposite the main entrance to the school. I had not taken much notice of the building but as we walked to it I saw the discreet notice 'Oben Ohne'. My German was good enough to understand that it meant 'nothing on top'. We spent a funny couple of hours drinking good wine and a meal of venison and being waited on by topless waitresses who had obviously been briefed to ensure that I had a good send off. My lasting thoughts of the men I met in Hannover, was that I was glad they are on our side!

My posting order to BAOR arrived and I saw that my next appointment was to be Second in Command of the Dusseldorf Provost Company—ironic, as I had been the RSM there at one time. It was basically an administrative post but in comfortable surroundings. I did not feel too guilty just having spent much of the last two years sleeping on the ground. On a Tuesday just before Christmas in 1981 I got a message from the orderly sergeant that said, "Get yourself over to the Assistant Provost Marshal's Office in the Headquarter block as he wants you straight away." Christ, I thought, I wonder what I have done? I moved fairly quickly to the office of Lt Col John Curtin, our APM at the time, and I knocked on the door and entered. He looked at me and said, "I have got to talk to you about something." I thought, well, here it comes, I knew that I was not too pure as things went; perhaps something had caught up with me. Suddenly Colonel John thrust out his hand and said, "Congratulations Roy, you have been awarded the MBE for your tour with 6 Field Force!"

I was speechless. I could not think of anything to say. Colonel John offered me a glass of sherry which I cannot remember drinking. I was so pleased that the award had come from that remarkable family of maroon berets that was my satisfaction and remains so to this day.

My family and I went to see the Queen in March 1981 at Buckingham Palace where indeed it was a great privilege to exchange a few words with Her Majesty. There it was, the culmination of my career, and to say that mum and dad were pleased is an understatement. We had a bad journey on the way home to Kent where in sixty miles we lost two windscreens in my Volkswagen Beetle that brought the kids to tears, as they were frightened. I hoped that was not an omen.

Back to Germany for a while and then it was return to the UK to downtown Brixton in Upper Tulse Hill in London to run 253 Provost Company RMP, a TAVR unit with a BAOR supportive role. The TA Centre was old and dusty but the unit personnel were some of the best, dedicated and extremely well trained soldiers I had met. One funny story is two of the unit sergeants were filling up the motorcycles at the local petrol station dressed in old overalls when up roars a pink American style motor with music pounding the area and four Rastafarians the worse for wear being on something or other. "Fill it up, honky tonk," says the driver to my man, mistaking him for the attendant. "Certainly sir," he replied and commenced to fill the car through the rear passenger window whilst my other colleague produced his cigarette lighter and commenced to flick the flame on and off. A contribution to the Lifeboat Fund would be appreciated, suggested my colleague. There was silence and a £10 note was produced. The RNLI was now better off and the Rasta's departed slowly as one did not want any sparks. We thought that there might be a repercussion from this but nothing ever came.

Whilst at Brixton I received an invitation to return to Dusseldorf to be the Second in Command of a parade to be held in the town of Xanten on the Rhine. The 101st Provost Company, Royal Military Police, were to receive the 'Freedom of the City' award on the 11th September 1982. This practice of granting the honorary freedom of the city dates back to the early Roman Empire and those who have earned this distinction are honoured for their excellent services and in recognition of the trust, confidence and friendship which exists between the two parties. In March 1945 this military unit took part in the opposed River Rhine crossing at Xanten and following the assault established its headquarters in the town and thus began the relationship that exists to today.

I made my way to Dusseldorf where we practiced our parade format which included the right to march through the town, with swords drawn, bayonets fixed and bands playing. We trooped a framed scroll bearing the joint insignia and signed by the Burgermeister and the Provost Marshal of the Army. We were well received by the townsfolk of Xanten and the parade was held in glorious weather. The toasts were never ending and the speeches went on and on in the council chambers of the Rathaus (Town Hall). It was a tired and slightly tipsy contingent that made their way back to Dusseldorf. I believe I am entitled to free rides on the buses and, once a year, coffee and cakes with the Burgermeister!

My time at Brixton was shortened with the surprise promotion to Major, Officer Commanding, 156 Provost Company at Colchester in Essex. I knew that I could have opted for the popular quartermaster role, which would have allowed me to go on to Lieutenant Colonel, but I wanted to be given my own independent command, as these were rare for officers commissioned from the ranks. This appointment coupled with my award of the MBE completely satisfied my ambitions. The Provost Marshal commented on this at my dining out from the Corps in that having been promoted ten times was a most unusual achievement. He had researched the records and could only find one other—'a Major Fletcher'—who matched my exceptional career. It was during this time of reflection that I felt that I had done my bit. I had had a full career and was satisfied in full.

After my first year I started to think about the rest of my life and what to do. Stay in the Army? There is nothing worse than an old soldier, so I started to look around for something that would interest me and bring me the job satisfaction that I now needed. What the hell does a 30-year military man do? My days were filled with some uncertainty as I began to contemplate a new life. I confided in my second in command, Captain Ian Waters. Ian was a mature man who had joined the Army late for his years and was enthusiastically trying to make up for lost time, whereas I was considering doing the opposite. His advice was good and I found to my embarrassment he was always right! He was one of the few who actually agreed with my thoughts. Whilst not wanting to lose a friend and colleague he trusted, I am pleased to say that he went on to become one of the finest officers that our Corps had seen and indeed also achieved his ambition before taking up a civilian appointment. He was right as usual!

Whilst sitting in the comfortable leather chairs in the Officer's Mess in Colchester I began to read the employment vacancies sections of all the national newspapers each day. I found that for every "general employment" post advertised there were hundreds of applicants like myself and the competition was fierce. I trawled through the old boy network, making it known that I would soon be looking for a job, when out of the blue an ex-Corps member working for Racal Chubb Security Systems Limited rang me and asked me to drop over for a chat. I was suffering from a slipped disc at this time and had spent a while in hospital in Woolwich, which did not bode well for any medical examination. My back mended enough for me to attend an interview in Feltham where I met the Chief Sales Executive who said he had an opportunity in West Africa that might suit me—was I interested? What to do? 30 years in the Army—stay or go? My next post would be most probably to command the 160 Provost Company RMP, in Aldershot, where I had already served. No, damn it, now was the time to continue to fill my life with a new challenge and the money was extremely attractive. I knew that I would be well off what with my military pension and gratuity plus the overseas earnings that were tax-free. I decided that I would resign and have a crack at this new venture in, where was it, Ghana? I knew nothing about West Africa except basic details and I had never served in Africa or visited that vast continent. I was an innocent. I did not know what to expect and perhaps if I had, I may not have gone there!

I tendered my resignation, much to the horror of some of my close friends who thought I was stark raving mad. Why change something you knew like the back of your hand for something unknown and far away? Now I think that we were both right. Either way would have been good for me, but the spirit of adventure had by now got into my system. It was difficult walking out of the barracks at Colchester not being able to return in the privileged appointment I had left and being exposed now to a new world without the total support I had enjoyed left me feeling insecure. My next step was off to Feltham to finish my resettlement period with Racal Chubb Security Systems Limited and the preparation for the contract in West Africa.

My family and my close friends were now mixed in their feelings for my actions. It seems strange to myself that whatever would be, would be. In 1956, in a miserable barrack room in Inkerman Barracks, Woking, in Surrey, a song made popular by Doris Day was played frequently on our radio and I likened it to the current time that I was now experiencing. Somewhere in my mental system something had to be satisfied, and this was the time. The 1956 song "Que Sera Sera, Whatever Will Be Will Be" had worked for me and there was no reason that it would not continue in that way. One of my dearest friends said to me, "If you fell in a bucket of camel shit you would always come out smelling of violets!" To date, that has always been so—long may it continue!

Fortunately there was not a lot of time to think too clearly. Wrapping up one's life's post career administration and preparing for the new unknown world in a few days created so many 'what ifs', 'buts' and 'maybes', and really there were not many answers forthcoming. My troublesome back was not 100% fit and the thought of something going wrong was always uppermost in the mind. It was too late to turn the clock back now—one had to carry on. I was not to know that the humid heat of Africa would be kind to my ailing discs and that it would be the best therapy there was outside of a hot salt-water hospital spa bath.

The die had been cast. This irrevocable step was now to be set in motion. There was just the first feeling of loneliness and a little insecurity creeping in. The big military family was not there to turn to any more—Bishop, you are now on your own!

PROJECT 3072

I was accommodated in bed and breakfast rooms in Feltham near to the Racal Chubb offices where I was to attend as part of my Army resettlement training. This is a scheme to assist all servicemen leaving the forces to prepare them for their civilian employment, probably one of the Army's best schemes. I was pleased to see that I would be enjoying not only my Army pay during this time but my salary from Racal Chubb would also be paid. This double bubble payment would continue until my final date on the Army's payroll on 13th February 1986. Paddy Baker and I sat down to plan our action for the coming contract time, he being the Contract Manager and I would hold the appointment of Chief Instructor. Together we would provide training and the writing of all procedures for an integrated security force for the Volta River Authority for the protection of their hydroelectric plans on the River Volta and other land-based installations.

The security force eventually would be as many as 300 men, but first we had to create and include the selection of a Chief Security Officer and his managers to whom we would hand over the reins on completion of our contract. In the 1960s the Ghanaian Government had offered the American VALCO consortium the opportunity to develop the Volta River Project with very attractive terms. This project was hoped to become the keystone of Ghana's economic development. It would provide large quantities of electricity, supplies and power to an aluminium smelting plant, and would promote the opening of mines, a harbour at Tema, railways and roads. My learning curve continued and I found that our work would be at the first huge dam at Akosombo at the southern tip of Lake Volta. It was also the main operational base, thence down river to Akuse where the Kpong Dam stood and where the VRA training school is also located, and finally down to the sea at Tema where there are workshops, stores and port facilities.

The Volta River Authority is the jewel in the crown for Ghana, being the showpiece for all visiting heads of state and international bodies, and also contained the presidential country retreat for the head of state. The current security force was small and ageing and needed an urgent upgrading, increase in numbers and the placing of a new management team. The planned installation of CCTV surveillance systems, electronic turnstiles and intruder alarm measures required us to recruit and train a high calibre of guard who would in return receive enhanced pay and benefits for their labour. I was informed that there was an eager number of volunteers for this employment but I did not realise that would bring its own problems. The threat against the Volta River Authority was in the main major theft of stores and equipment, which were always in short supply. Even a small theft could interrupt the production of hydroelectric power. Every commodity was precious in these isolated areas; even if it was a quantity of oil that was extracted from the working plant, it may take several days to replace it. The terrorist threat always existed, but confined in the main to border areas where the Ghanaian Army dealt with incursions fairly severely. There it was. Train a security force and hand it over to the host nation. Two men on a shoestring—I think that's how it looked.

My contract for this project was short and simple; I was to be the chief instructor for one year on an unaccompanied basis with effect from 20th January 1986. The contract was subject to a fitness examination. I was concerned as my back was not too sound, but I passed. My salary was generous, needless to say. The overseas allowance was £14,000 alone and that was good money in 1986. The money would be paid in 12 monthly instalments into a UK bank of my choice. Income tax was to be my responsibility and in the end it worked out well with no tax liability. My working hours were whatever was required by the contract. Holidays came in the form of two one-month periods: one halfway through the contract, and one at the end were normal with free economy air tickets being paid by the Company. British Caledonian mostly covered travel to Ghana with flights from Gatwick departing on Tuesdays and Fridays and returns on Wednesdays and Saturdays, the flight duration being about 7½ hours. The African World Travel Services were based in Regent Street, London, and was the main booking office. The cost was £489: it was always best to have a prepaid return ticket in your possession should there ever be a need for a quick exit!

Accommodation in Ghana would be free. I had to find my own food, but an allowance was built into the salary. A third party insurance policy would be maintained on my behalf. If I required medical treatment, this would be paid for by the company, and if there was a serious illness or accident I would be flown to the nearest suitable hospital. Should I wish to terminate there was a 90 day notice period. I signed my contract on 20th January 1986 and flew out to Ghana the following day. As I had a beer on the evening of the 20th I thought, bloody hell—what have I done?

WHAT HAVE I DONE?

Flight departure was from Gatwick. I was still unprepared for what was about to confront me and like a lamb to the slaughter went I. I had considerable excess baggage with me containing the multi-various training aids I had collected and, what with two suitcases and various bits, I was somewhat overloaded. I rang home for the last time and was reassured by my wife that everyone was pleased that I had left the Army and was looking forward to seeing how things went. I thought in my innocence that I would be ringing home shortly after arrival to bring them up to date. Boy, was I wrong! The flight was enjoyable—the British Caledonian aircraft was full of noisy and happy Ghanaians returning home, some businessmen travelling on to other destinations, and I noted a number of quiet males, mature and tanned, who really did not contact anyone. I decided it was time for a 'pick me up' of Mrs Bells, that favourite amber liquid of mine which cures bites, the common cold and does not give me any blood pressure. I fell asleep, having lugged so many boxes around airports, worrying about the next step at Accra and trying to come to terms with myself. I awoke to find a very young Ghanaian having a pee up my leg nearest the aisle. This refreshed me. I chatted to his parents until it was time for the descent to Accra Airport.

From the windows I could not see a great deal—a few lights, but generally total darkness. When the pilot announced we would be landing soon at Accra the aircraft was full of applause from the passengers and some even began to sing. I thought this cannot be too bad. People began standing in the aisles, despite all the standard warning light systems; this was a noisy musical homecoming that was beyond the control of the cabin staff. I decided just to sit tight and go with the flow. Hell men, this is obviously Africa!

There was a scramble to leave the plane and the stewardesses had to let the people go their way and surprisingly we were soon inside the terminal building. Africa struck me with its heat, even though this was midnight; the humidity stuck my shirt to my body, the warm and not unpleasant smell of people, blossoms and overripe drains. I was surrounded by smiling black faces trying to help me. Thank God Paddy appeared with a group of uniformed men who shooed away some of my helpers. Customs and passport control was fairly quick. It was at this time, with so much baggage to look after, that I needed eyes in my backside. I had not reached the group of VRA men to carry anything and I had my Irish blackthorn cane stolen. Some very quick thief snatched it away and it was gone; despite my later offering a substantial reward, it was never recovered. I gave the lady customs officer some bars of Imperial soap and the passport officer a £5 note tip and I was through!

Paddy and I shook hands; he was half pissed but still operating. The Ghanaian security officers, the acting superintendent, his right-hand man and two drivers, stared at me and I looked at them. Africans can read a white man very quickly, whereas it is not so the other way. I deliberately looked into their eyes and held their extended hands firmly and respectfully. I meant to continue as I started, come what may. It had worked for thirty years in the British Army and there was no reason why it should not remain that way.

After loading we drove to our Dutch agents' guesthouse nearby where I spent the night in a spartan room but still unprepared for the shocks to follow. In the morning we had coffee and fruit served by the lovely Helen who giggled constantly. We then left for the agents' building only a few hundred metres away. The offices were in a single five-storey building with the Standard Bank on the ground floor and Reiss & Co occupying most of the remainder. I met Rick, the Dutch agent, who was a huge man with hands like meatloaves. I gathered that Reiss & Co managed and coordinated many companies' contracts, acting as a reporting centre and administrative support team for other contractors like ourselves. One thing did puzzle me—we deposited £800 individually with Reiss and Co for 'emergencies'—was this running money, or what? We drew on our funds when we needed them and received any balance before we left. Reiss & Co had a regular telex link with Chubb in the UK and we passed reports as and when needed and received instructions in return. The time had come to travel to Akuse where Paddy told me we had a temporary bungalow to share until our individual bungalows were ready. This seemed fine, but the truth would be apparent when we arrived.

We set off from Accra in two vehicles. Paddy had been given a Peugeot 405 and our VRA security truck followed. Accra is surrounded by controlled police checkpoints on all routes in and out of the city. We approached our checkpoint at a speed which I winced at. Sarpong, the driver whom I had yet to get to know, was showing off and feeling 'important' so he tried to go straight through without stopping. When I had the muzzle of a rusty sten gun placed in my car window I thought, "Oh shit." The police were not happy. Who the hell was driving and who was in charge? There followed a discussion between all parties with the result that I produced a receipt from the passport office where they had retained my passport and this seemed to satisfy the Inspector in charge. I do not think he could read, but he gained face from this paper and allowed us to go.

As we left the police checkpoint I wondered whether that rusty sten would have worked as it had certainly seen better days. Paddy cynically said the police wanted a 'dash' (a bribe or tip) as they were so poorly paid. As we travelled I thought it was a misty or foggy day as visibility was poor now that we were out in the countryside. I questioned this and was told it was 'harmatan' season when sand clouds came down from the Sahara and cloaked West Africa in dust. This was only seasonal and would clear in a few weeks but it certainly marred my first impressions. The bush, the countryside, was flat, covered in small trees and large bushes. The soil was an orange brown. There were few travellers and those I saw were in ramshackle cars and trucks held together by God knows what. They were overloaded with people hanging precariously onto the sides with bundles on their laps. The road was full of potholes so one drove in a zigzag fashion to miss them. This system resulted in many fatal accidents. Along the roadside we passed stalls selling tomatoes and onions and not much else. Little did I know that these stalls would provide me with most of my daily diet.

The drive then continued at a fairly high rate of knots, mostly, I think, to impress the roadside onlookers. Personally, I was a little concerned at this headlong rush for no reason. As we reached our destination I saw that the country was fairly flat but with a couple of hills on our right, outside Akuse. I was to learn that these hills were sacred and had housed natives defying the growing British influence in the past. I became fond of those two lumps.

We reached Akuse, a dull uninteresting group of single storey buildings with everything run down and in the afternoon even the trees seemed to have died in the heat of the day. We saw little or no one on our arrival. We drove to our temporary bungalow that had two-bedrooms, a small kitchen, bathroom and living room with cane furniture and was very basic with a garden at the rear and views as far as you could see in the seasonal fog. Augustine was the houseboy—smart and well mannered, but a bit too smooth for me as he said he had worked for hotels and rich people.

My bedroom was the first shock. No one had told me I needed bed linen. All that was there was a mattress on an iron bedstead, a chest of drawers and a bedside table. I slept under my dressing gown on a mattress that had seen better times. It was quite a while before I could find sheets and pillows. The toilet functioned sometimes, and one had to become accustomed to unflushed conditions. The shower worked when there was water available and this seemed to be intermittent. Meals were when we could buy something. There were eggs for breakfast with local bread, and at evening time fish and local vegetables, mostly yams. My weight plummeted and I looked slim and healthy—but hungry as a bear. I noted that Paddy was taking pleasure in my discomfort; he could have warned me about the simple necessities of life, but I did not give him the pleasure of ever voicing a single complaint. I went to bed during those early days thinking, "What have I done?" As I lay there I managed to count my earnings to date and thought, "Keep it going, Toby."

Initially, I found that I could not understand this cloud-shrouded land with its absence of accepted modern facilities such as roads, railways, telephone systems and the hundred and one life support conveniences we enjoy in the West. I was going to have to learn things the hard way and slowly take my time.

GHANA

In the time I had during my resettlement course and bedtime reading, then later on my flight and during the first few days, I tried to put together what I knew about Ghana. In my layman's knowledge I now knew that the Republic of Ghana had a population of about 30 million and was the first British colony in the sub-Saharan Africa to gain independence in 1957. Its recent history had been one of intermittent military rule with the country being run by Flight Lieutenant Gerry Rawlings. In the 1980s Ghana's Provisional National Defence Council (PDNC), under Gerry Rawlings, made an economic recovery programme backed by the World Bank and IMF, and this included work to restore their road network which had fallen into disrepair. Ghana enjoys good relations with the West, which provides most of Ghana's military and development aid. The country enjoys two rainy seasons: April to July and September to November, and generally the climate is humid, hot but acceptable. The people are interesting and come from various cultural groups; the largest is the Akan who include the Ashanti and Fanti peoples. Other important groups are the Mole Dagbani in the North and the Ga Adangbe around Accra and Ewe in the South East.

There are few tribal tensions and the family ties are strong. Cocoa is their main crop, which is cheap to produce, and accounts for 15% of the world total. Gold and Bauxite are major exports. Production of these two products and diamonds and manganese are important resources, which will continue to be expanded. The cutting of wood for fuel, timber, has damaged the environment and farming has destroyed a large percent of the forests and has caused serious pollution. There is not a major crime problem and corruption is less of a problem than years ago. Education is popular with all systems being over subscribed and the few high quality boarding schools and four universities are at bursting point.

English is the national language with some eight other local languages. Ghana is a religious land with over 40% of the people being Christians of varying beliefs, as I was to find later in my travels and when I became a member of one of their churches. I found that the main diet of the land was cassava, rice, bananas, oil palm, coconuts, limes, yams and corn maize. Fishing satisfies 75% of the people's eating needs. There is meat to be found by the hunters but this gets less every year. Vegetables from the markets are in evidence and, for the fortunate ones, commodities such as we enjoy at home. This is a land where food is not wasted. The health of the people I considered to be generally good as public hygiene has improved rather than improvements in medical care. The more I learnt of this fascinating land inspired me to contribute something whilst I was a guest in Ghana.

Mention must be made of the risk to one's health in this land of some 70 degrees, which is responsible for a lot of nasty problems. I think malaria is the highest risk, which kills thousands of all ages. I remember when I visited the Chief Executive in Accra he said make sure you take your anti-malaria tablets. Around such a place as a freshwater lake, of course, mosquitoes were rampant. In the evening time you could almost hear them revving up like squadrons of fighters ready to take off and bite you. I was lucky—for some reason they never touched me. I put it down to showering in the local water with a whisky mix. The Larium anti-malaria tablets, one a week, had a side effect of massive depression. I went back to the well-tested Paludrin tablets twice a day. They made you look a bit yellow but you got by. The medical check-up on my guards revealed that TB was a major problem. A host of dirty water complaints always affected the children. There was a nasty little worm-like water pest called Bilharzia that gets into your bowel or bladder and causes internal bleeding. I saw a lot of this. The message was, keep out of still freshwater pools where they thrived. Smallpox, sleeping sickness and the lack of available treatments took its toll on the local inhabitants.

Although AIDS was rife in East and South Africa, I was not aware of it in my area. Maybe, as we were off the beaten track, there was less chance of the spread of the disease. I do remember my guys joking about people who were skinny and they said that they had 'slim'—their nickname for AIDS. Life expectancy was about 50 years in the villages, unless you were lucky. So there it was, the odds were stacked against you if you lived in a mud hut and lived hand to mouth off the land. If one dwelt on the risks that one could meet, there would never be any visitors to West Africa.

There was a noticeable lack of animals—no horses, no cattle, some goats and the occasional pig farm. The tsetse fly, a hornet-like insect, being the worst enemy of domestic animals, farming was done by hand and no ploughing using oxen or horses. I wonder why they didn't use tractors. Flies cannot bite metal machines, but I was soon to find out. Farm machinery was far beyond the pocket of the farmers. There was evidence of old rusty Russian tractors which had been donated in the past, but like all things, no spares, no fuel, no more aid money, and they remained as a memorial to the many lost and failed projects. I even saw a failed North Korean fish farm.

At Akosombo there was a medical centre donated by the Swedish Government. It was complete in all aspects with a mini-operating room and a dental annex. The problem was there was not a drug in the place and what medicine there was, was out of date and, despite the efforts of the UK-trained doctor, was pretty hopeless.

Sarpong, our driver, complained of toothache one day. I think he must have had a fight as his face was swollen and he had bumps and bruises to go with it. One of his teeth was broken off and he was in great pain. He had been chewing on some local medicine for a couple of days, but this wasn't working so he opted to see the dentist. I was with him when the doctor who doubled up as the dentist put him in the nice new chair and extracted the tooth without anaesthetic. I saw a tear roll down his cheek, but he didn't cry out. He spat blood and I paid the doctor for his services. I also dashed Sarpong 20,000 Cedis (about £2) for his bravery. It was odd seeing what had happened in a fully equipped surgery down to the latest instruments. This reinforced my fear about what would happen if I were ill or injured! On the way back to Akuse, Sarpong suddenly said, "The doctor cheated you. I am VRA—my treatment is free!" I had a feeling that Sarpong would be visiting the doctor and negotiating a share of the dental fees—that's how it goes.

Speaking of medical treatment, I became aware that my guards were visiting the local doctor, the medicine man, for treatment of their ailments. John Agameti came to work with his head shaven and covered in white clay. It was a mixture of ash from the fire and some soil that had been applied to cure his headaches. It was later found that he had a brain tumour and this caused his death. I am sure that some cures did work, but in the main death was the natural result of any serious illness. Nevertheless I'm convinced that the local 'traditional' doctors have a lot to offer; if I were at death's door, I would invite them to assist. After all, they've been around longer than our medics!

AKUSE—MY VILLAGE

Akuse had been around since times before history was written in any form in Ghana. It's a small village on the banks of the River Volta, and its peace was only interrupted by the arrival of the engineers to build the dams funded by International Aid. On the outskirts of the village the new arrivals built administrative offices, a training school and a substantial clubhouse and social centre with a swimming pool. Some new roads were created and bungalows built alongside the new lanes to house the engineers and their families. I understand they had mobile refrigerated food stores from where the basic necessities of life were available.

Since the completion of the project everything has fallen into a run-down condition. Families from the VRA have moved into the bungalows with a few expatriate whites also there, and the clubhouse facilities operated on a limited basis. The swimming pool was operational, generally with an attendant who insisted that one showered before entering the pool, even though once in the water you found you were sharing it with large frogs. Mind you, that led me to believe the water was unpolluted. Nevertheless, I tried not to swallow, though that was almost impossible. We would have long periods when the pool was closed and lay empty for days. You cannot put a full westernised system into Africa and expect it to work forever!

The village housing was a mixture of part brick and part wooden dwellings with most outhouses made of mud. The roadside drains ran green with stagnant water and the road itself was potholed to a dangerous level. There was a market from which a very limited amount of commodities were traded. Onions, tomatoes and sweet potatoes were sold from little tables with a flimsy roof covering them. I bought these food items, which supplemented my Heinz Beans and local bread. I passed on the scrawny chickens—sold live, of course. I found a cobbler in a little hut on stilts that proved useful later when my shoes rotted and the soles fell off. There was a beer stall where you could sit in the two privileged chairs and watch life go by. Paddy and I were sitting there on a weekend enjoying a warm beer when the bar owner attempted to sell us his two daughters who were a burden to him. It was with some regret we could not accept his offer as they were very attractive and we were still playing the white man's standards. The school had been built as part of the VRA project and was located near the clubhouse. On weekday mornings crocodiles of children would appear, each with a stool balanced on their heads, and make their way to lessons. They were all smartly dressed, well disciplined and eager to learn. Classroom furniture was their stools and benches. They boasted blackboards, chalk and a small library of books. The children wrote in trays of fine sand whilst practising the alphabet before going on to books and pencils. The standard of their basic education was higher than that at home here in the UK.

Akuse boasted a medical centre but only the ageing sign was any reassurance to those who were sick. I carried unfortunates to the centre, having found them in distressing conditions—only to find there were only poorly trained nurses on duty with no doctor immediately available. There were no medicines that I could see. There was a trolley to lie on and water to refresh the patient, but done in the most caring and sympathetic way I had ever seen. My respect for the ladies at the centre grew over the months I was there and it was to them I donated my medical supplies on my departure.

Elsewhere in this book I have told of the chapel; and in and around Akuse, there were several churches, all well attended on Sundays. The Bible took the place of food and wealth to comfort these patient people. Every Sunday morning an elderly man passed the front of my dwelling on his way to church. He carried his hymn book proudly and was dressed in a three-piece suit with no shirt or shoes, but my God he had dignity. I used to waylay him on his return to offer him a cup of tea and listened to his tales of when the British ran life in their colony. I gathered that he wished there were a re-colonisation of sorts, not to rule but to administer and provide all the basic communication services that were now no longer available. I remember him smiling wryly when talking about the old days. He said he could never understand why he was taught about the battle of Hastings in 1066!

Around the huddle of buildings that was Akuse were the small clearings where everyone tried to grow maize corn, but at this time the drought was killing everything and only a few cobs would be harvested. Fish from the Volta became the lifesaver for many a family. Opposite my bungalow were two similar dwellings where the ladies sold bread, cigarettes, sardines and other items. I used to purchase my small loaf of sweet white bread on alternate mornings so as to give them some income for good relationships. I felt protected in many ways by these two families who always kept an eye on me. The children from these houses, about a dozen, always greeted me in the mornings, holding my hands and clinging onto my clothes to the extent that I had difficulty in walking. They used to pinch my skin to see what a white man felt like. Whenever I had some sweets my friends quickly consumed them. It was a privilege to greet my young neighbours every day. I just thought I was doing the right thing and you never knew when you would need their help.

THE BUNGALOW

When we first drove to Akuse we were accommodated in a temporary bungalow with Paddy in one bedroom and I in the other. I have mentioned that it was spartan with some cane furniture and the very basics. The shower operated when there was water available, the toilets worked on the same basis, and the small kitchen had a small electric cooker and fridge. The absence of bedding and other comfort items did not thrill me. We were told that our individual bungalows would be ready soon and this would improve the quality of life. Living with a miserable and temperamental bachelor such as Paddy was not my scene. He seemed to have a love-hate relationship with Africa to extremes that were not in my world. Thank God the new bungalow became ready and I was able to live at my pace and do things my way.

Augustine, the houseboy who had looked after us in the old bungalow, continued to look after Paddy and I found myself another employee whose name was Kingsley. Kingsley was a devout Jehovah's Witness and very mild and quiet in manner. He was the hairiest person I have ever seen but nonetheless immaculate in his clothing and personal hygiene. He had little experience but he managed to turn over the washing to good effect and clean the bungalow, although it never really got dirty as I am a fairly tidy person. He used to make a sandwich lunch for me—normally three sardine sandwiches, sometimes with onion or tomato added—and make a cup of tea. This constituted my main lunch for a year. Whatever I wanted to eat in the evening I prepared myself. Normally it was tomato, beans and something, as there was never much meat available. Its funny, I could measure the days in a month by the number of bean tins I had in the cupboard! The renovated bungalow had the cane furniture, but this time there was some bedding and generally I felt better.

I heard Kingsley shout one lunchtime and he came running in, shouting, "Snake, snake!" He took me out to the washroom at the rear of the kitchen and there was my first hooded cobra with its neck dilated, ready to spit or strike. There was no way we could chase it out. I ran down the road to Alex Wysocki's bungalow and borrowed his 12-gauge shotgun from their houseboy. Back in the washroom the snake was angry and Kingsley was praying in the kitchen. I knew that I had little time to aim as the washroom was so small and the snake could easily spit over that distance or take a lunge at me. I fired both barrels: one a head shot, because it was the biggest target, and one a body shot. At that close range the cobra was almost blown to pieces and I saw that I had also blown a new ventilation hole in the washroom wall. My neighbours took the remnants of the snake away as Kingsley was still giving thanks for our deliverance.

We found that snakes were going to be a menace due to my neighbour keeping chickens and their eggs attracted all sorts of predators. When leaving the bungalow in the morning, you had to make the snake check to ensure there were none hanging in the porch area and then strike the pickup with a metal bar to dispel any unwelcome residents in the vehicle engine or cab area. I found that the areas surrounding Lake Volta were infested with snakes and creepy crawlies due to the rising water of the lake, which drove all such things in its path as it rose; this yielded areas of some five miles radius around the lake which were hostile to man and beast. I learned never to stroke the branches of overhanging trees as these housed the green mamba, beautiful in colour but deadly to man. It was best not to dwell on the subject of snakes too much as you could go mad. The one that frightened me particularly was the puff adder, a flat slug of a snake that looked hideous and struck at your ankles as you passed because it was too slow to scurry away like its counterparts. We ran over one in the truck and this did not help my courage when I saw the potential of its ugly fangs.

The bungalow had a porch, main living room, kitchen, shower room and two bedrooms that were more than adequate for me. The electricity functioned most of the time, which was reassuring as we were only a mile from the power station. The water supply was intermittent and what did come from the taps was not safe to drink. I made sure that I boiled the water and then added two purification tablets into the bottled water in the fridge. The garden around the bungalow had a hibiscus hedgerow which produced brilliant red flowers. There was some bougainvillea around the front porch coloured mauve and white with a couple of unknown evergreen bushes. There was no grass, just the hard baked earth that was swept by Kingsley. When I looked at these colours I could only think of the paradise and hell that was Africa.

Mention must be made of the march of the soldier ants. One evening I went for a pee in the toilet when I noticed large ants emerging from the floor wastewater drain that served the shower and also out of the hand basin plughole. I was not too aware of the threat of these creatures but decided to pour the last of my domestic disinfectant down both drains and thought no more of it. An hour later I heard swearing and cursing coming from Paddy's place next door and looked into his kitchen where he was furiously boiling water with every container he had. "Soldier ants!" he shouted. "There seems to be an infestation of them!" I picked up what powders I had for nasties and went to join him when I was stung badly on my lower legs and found I had stepped into the path of millions of ants travelling away from the side of my bungalow and entering the corner of Paddy's kitchen and out again through a rear window. The threat was that if they changed course they would travel through the entire length of the building. Our neighbours had heard our cries and came with more powders, but the march of the ants continued through boiling water, even fuel that was ignited, for as soon as the flames died they came on again.

I saw them building bridges with their own dead and living to continue their passage. I was thanking my lucky stars that they did not like my disinfectant and their scouts had decided to take an easier route. If I had not gone for a pee their route would have dissected my residence. We finally diverted their travel by a number of us sweeping their marching column to pass along the rear of Paddy's place from where they then entered a hole under the concrete road and disappeared. It took some time to clear up, but at least we kept them out. It was eerie as you could actually hear them passing during the night, like the sound of small sticks being moved by the wind. In the morning they were gone, but their trail remained about four inches wide and smooth like a wheel track. I did not sleep much as the thought was there that they might have another try. I saw nature at its best but it was not for the faint hearted. From that day I rarely ventured into my back garden as it was overgrown and full of who knows what might be there crawling and slumbering in the sunshine.

My final thought was never go into the garden unless absolutely necessary.

RECRUITING AND TRAINING THE NEW SECURITY FORCE

Our office, from where we would run the recruiting and training, was a small room on the end of the fire section building. It was some 9' x 9' and contained two small desks, two chairs, a manual typewriter and a notice board. There was a side door to a covered porch style area that would be the office for the clerical support of two clerks from VRA, which was part of the agreement. Alfred Tordzro was our chief clerk, an experienced man, and he was assisted by a typist and general help—Emmanual Levor, who had the misfortune to try and read Paddy's manuscript writings of the new procedures and security officer's handbook. He was terrified of Paddy who exploded frequently, but he soldiered through. We had a single air conditioning unit in the wall that worked occasionally. This, then, was the hub of the project.

During my tour of the training school I went into the engineer's office and there on the wall was a full-scale plan of the electricity generating station at Sellindge that was only some four miles from my home back in England. What a small world. Mr Torkorno had studied in the UK and had been based at Sellindge for six months. I had probably passed him in the street in Ashford, never thinking that one day I would see him in Ghana. He kindly marked my house location on his plan and it became a talking point for him when he received visitors.

The VRA training school was some 1000 metres down the road towards the Kpong Dam. I was lucky that the Army had taught me to type because the old Olympia typewriter was used for producing test papers and our correspondence. If you wanted copies you had to use the old carbon paper that was available, and if you wanted to photocopy something it was a long trip to where the few copiers could be found. From my brief I saw that training time had been allocated for two weeks for officers and supervisors and three weeks for the guards. The training would include the old chestnuts—dress, discipline, local law, VRA Organisation, First Aid, Radio Communications, Fire and Accident Prevention, security duties and familiarisation visits to sites. The bulk of the training would be my responsibility with help from Paddy and a few VRA specialists.

The equipment training would be the most difficult part of the familiarisation activity. This included fibre optic cables for the walls of the central stores at Tema, turnstile "full-o-stile" gates for the dam at Akosombo, and the stores at Teme. Then there were the VRM 4540 SXU radio systems at the presidential guesthouse, panic alarm buttons, CCTV monitors throughout most of the sites, and anti-climb outrigger defences in most locations. Surprisingly, the guards quickly took on board the basic operating methods and did not seem too awed by the amount of technology due to be installed. This is where we had to get our recruiting right in order that the student could cope academically with this mass of new security aids and be at least trained to an operator level. The Chief Security Officer would in due course complete a more sophisticated training schedule in the UK in preparation to help guide his force members.

The aim was to train the officers and supervisors first so that they could then be co-opted as junior instructors as the training progressed, and with this in mind be in a position to undertake the continuation training on our departure. The names of the officers and supervisors were given to us by the VRA Personnel Director. I noted that there was a requirement for some weeding out of those now too old or ill, but no one had the wish to do this unenviable task and wanted us to do it for them. I felt that this was a tribal or family problem that was best done by a stranger. There were two officers and supervisors courses and in the main they went well. The students were intelligent and knew that their jobs were on the line. As we expected, the foot drill and patrolling exercises produced the first of several very mature individuals who dropped out despite their best efforts and their inability to cope was duly reported and they were pensioned off. From the dozen seniors there emerged the future officers and managers who were fairly and honestly reported on and you could see that their confidence was on the increase. So much for the officers. They, in fact, were the easiest to take on board the new systems and for us to train.

Each guard course was planned to have ten students. Now came the problem. The VRA personnel department always sent twelve. We were requested to test the twelve students and select the best ten for training, which was unfair on both parties. I hoped we were not going to become the hatchet men of the VRA, but it certainly looked like it. The test for gaining a place on the course was some general knowledge questions on Ghana, some simple arithmetic, dictation from the local paper and a two-minute oral presentation on why they wanted to be a security officer. It was difficult at times to select the lucky ten, but we did it. Then came the disappointment of the two losers—they were absolutely disappointed, even going to the lengths of falling on their knees and embracing our legs, begging to be allowed to remain. This was emotion I had never before seen. This scene repeated itself throughout the time of our project. Uniforms were issued by the stores department and in the main were functional. The guards did not enjoy wearing boots and in the classroom I used to find three lines of boots parked by the desks after we had returned from the first drill lesson of the day. The three weeks training was conducted on a Monday to Friday basis, leaving Saturday mornings for Paddy and I to catch up with our paperwork. Each day started with drill on the concrete flat top of the Kpong Dam. The sun rose behind a barrier wall and shielded us a little so that the sweat did not run too much. We taught foot drill up to saluting on the march, to halt and salute and how to conduct the basic morning parade. The guards took easily to drill; like their dancing and singing, it came naturally. Mr Miller helped me with the drill and the pair of us used to demonstrate each movement before the guards tried it. To my amazement each time Mr Miller and I did a reasonable movement, the guards would break into applause and shout complimentary noises. What do you do? This is Africa, man! Just so long as we ensured the movement was correct, I was happy.

How my guards managed to arrive at the start of the day clean and tidy, pressed shirts and clean boots, I will never know. Some had travelled miles to get there and they had no transport. In fact, I think they walked. During the mid-morning break at 10:30 it was teatime in the training school. I supplied the tea bags, the duty student boiled the water and we all had black tea with no additives. Sometimes, if we were out on perimeter patrols which included drawing a plan of the sites and later writing a report, I used to stop at the roadside stalls and buy two bananas each for all eleven of us; then we would sit for a while and rest our feet because I insisted we did all this training on foot. During one patrol on the borders of the Kpong rice farm land, while we were pushing our way through tall grasses and bushes and were for a while out of sight of anything, I heard a warning shout behind me. I was on point with a very long stick striking the undergrowth to chase off any snakes, and heard Mr Mensah shouting: "Mad dog, mad dog—he is coming!" I immediately thought of rabies and worse, and set off at the run, also being propelled from behind by ten frightened men. Out of the bushes we came like a rocket, and there was the Greek manager of the farm whistling for his Doberman whose name was Sally! I hadn't realised that Africans have an inherent fear of dogs anyway and this helped propel my guards forward, taking me with them in their panic. This fear, plus the thought of becoming a rabies victim, was enough to make everybody move very quickly, whatever the heat and bush conditions were.

For a while we were known as the fastest foot patrol in the VRA. I was just relieved that we had not been harmed. The men on the course now had something in common and we made good progress without any further mishap. Mr Mensah was awarded five duty students for frightening his colleagues, much to the joy of the rest of the team. It was interesting to see how his morale improved. I heard them making woofing noises at Mr Mensah when he was around. Funnily enough, at the final course examination, Mr Mensah came out best in the class.

The heat in the afternoon plays havoc with the training. It was so hot that even the trees seemed to die and then come alive again as the sun went down. The training continued working like a sausage machine—Paddy writing the standing operating procedures day in and day out, myself becoming robotic-like, but I knew that we were achieving our aim.

Nearing the end of one training course, we did a perimeter patrol of Kpong rice farm. The sun scorched us and our shirts hung like wet clothes on our upper bodies. The grass was brown and dead and lizards scuttled away from us into the bushes and many times you jumped like hell as you thought it might be a snake of sorts. I took my usual place in the lead of the patrol, swiping at the grass from side to side to chase off unwelcome reptiles. I heard my guys talking behind me. They were basically saying it wouldn't hurt their bosses to get off their backsides and do what I was doing. They lacked leadership in a big way. As we reached the furthermost corner of the cultivated fields I found that a 40 metre section of the perimeter fence was missing, including the upright metal poles. This section of fencing had been carefully removed from where it entered a bushy area to where it exited back onto open ground. My guards said nothing but prowled around trying to look as if they were investigating the theft. I asked Mr Mensah what he thought. He looked at me and said, "This has been taken for domestic use." I could find no reply for this excellent response in such perfect English, but I wondered what he meant. I was to find my answer a few weeks later when I had to pick up Mr Mensah from his home for a one-off night guarding the Presidential guesthouse. I accepted his invitation to take some tea with his family and he was particularly keen to show me his new son. There, lying on a single bed, was a lovely young baby boy gurgling away and smiling—and suddenly I found my fence, part of which was now a single bed and home for Mr Mensah's new child. He knew I had spotted the freshly cut metal legs and said nothing. I shook his hand and complimented him and whispered, "When you have him christened, name him after me"—and he nodded. That remained my secret with Mr Mensah who proved his loyalty in many ways. Anyway, you cannot let a newborn baby sleep on the ground, can you?

When my class assembled for their foot drill the next morning I wished them good morning and hoped they had had a good night's sleep, some more comfortably than others, and their smiles told me all I needed to confirm that my guys had nicked the fence and broken it down into single bed frames for their families. I did not report my findings but just kept this ace up my sleeve should I need to play it. I asked myself the question: "Where is the line between duty and family when there is a need?" We replaced the fence by planting thorny bushes that were more effective than man-made defences.

Final examination day and the pass out parade was always a good day. The families came to see their loved ones march up and down and basically they did a good job because they were showing off. Pass certificates were presented; these had been printed for me at the Military Corrective Training Centre in Colchester for a small charge and part of their printing training for the inmates. The pass certificates were very popular and, in fact, I have seen one years on for a security officer working for a major UK company. I would like to have known how useful the certificate was. The course photographs, with everyone wearing a medal, were produced by Paddy, and these I handed out as gifts later.

Some days as we trained I was aware that we were being monitored by three men who seemed to turn up wherever we were. I had a feeling they were government security men keeping an eye on us, as these were turbulent times in the political struggle for power. I was even more convinced when I read an article in the *Ghanaian Times* where a 'Major Bishop' and a group of mercenaries had been intercepted at sea on a ship full of weapons bound from South Africa to Ghana. Perhaps this was why the immigration office had retained my passport every time I entered the country. Bishop is a common name and I am sure the Ghanaian Government had access to the British Army List to check me out. Perhaps this was the reason the security force was refused its application to be armed and, looking back, I'm glad that this was so. I thought I knew the government observer, a white man of unkempt appearance who, every time I saw him, was armed. He motored around the bush in an old German jeep that was in immaculate mechanical condition. He always had a girl with him and treated them like slaves. I never felt comfortable when I spotted him but knew he was in the employ of some organisation. He was a very odd man who frightened the locals who would not talk about him.

The training requirements came to an end and the force was looking good. Dressed in their new uniforms they were trained and keen to put their knowledge to use. I wondered how effective they would be when they came up against family and tribal connections. You never can tell in Africa. Paddy attended a selection board at the VRA Headquarters in Electro-Volta House in Accra to select the new Chief Security Officer. There were some eleven candidates and after two days' deliberations, an ex-Ghanaian Army Officer from their Education Corps was offered the job—a very intelligent man with no serious connections with the VRA, a fact that would give him a good start. This decision did not go down well with the acting Chief Security Officer who had been holding things together for a while, but he did become the second in command and was given a public commendation, which helped to overcome his loss of face. It's a small world as the following year when I was employed as the Ship's Security Officer for P&O Ferries at Dover, my office door opened and there stood the Ghana VRA Chief Security Officer! He was on a fairly punishing tour of UK sites as part of his training and had decided to say hello to an old friend. I'm not sure what my colleagues made of the embracing and the welcoming dance steps!

A young lance corporal on exercise near Sennelager in 1959

Batchelor days in Bielefeld, West Germany.
The Corporals' Mess—no ladies allowed in 1958!

Wedding day—18th May, 1959, at Christchurch in Ashford, Kent

Todtesheim—Danish/German Border in 1978.
6 Field Force on exercise in Northern Germany in their Nato Role

'The Office' attached to the Fire Station. Note the leaning pole—once there were telephone services.

Roy Bishop, still shaken and still stirred—0900 hours, just after the first drill session on a Monday morning.

My Toyota pickup which arrived late in the contract, but an absolute essential bit of kit for carrying the guards and equipment.

Children of the fishing village Odumasi, where all the men were named after the fishermen who followed Christ. I managed to buy some goggles and snorkels when on my first break in the UK and had great pleasure in giving them to two young fishermen, Matthew and Peter, who seemed to be the main suppliers of Volta Perch to their community.

On the balcony of the Volta Hotel at Akasombo. There is no food available, only green bottles of beer. The view was interesting if you could see through the last of the Harmatan mists due to lift in March when a spring-like season occurs. Buzzards and kites wheel above the hotel, kept aloft by hot thermals whilst they scan the ground for their next meal. Still wondering what the hell I had done!

My bungalow, which looks good from the outside with its two vehicles nearby.
It was functional and the rain did not come in, though the snakes did.
Surprisingly, the mosquitoes did not.

My house sign and the dustbin which never filled up! There is no waste in Africa; if you put something in the bin, it was not there the following day. I never saw a food item ever thrown away. Perhaps we could learn from that when you see what we do at home in the UK.

My neighbours who lived opposite my bungalow. Each morning and evening I was greeted by them, and this made life more worthwhile!

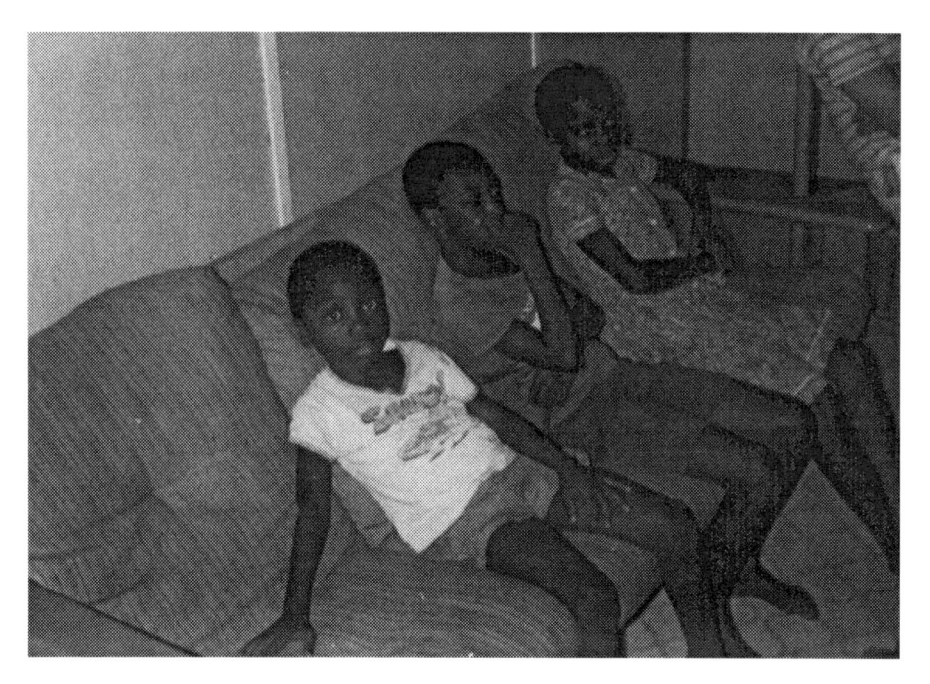

John and his sisters, who seemed to just walk in and out when they wished.
They trusted us completely and we were welcomed by their parents into the community.

Paddy conducting security survey training at the Akasombo Dam—the heat this day was over 90 degrees F.

Drill at dawn—on the top of the Akuse (Kpong) Dam when the sun is still rising and we are sheltered from the new day's heat. Mr Miller is acting drill instructor and the guys have just mastered saluting on the march.

Vehicle check point training at Akasombo, on the approaches to the Presidential residence—the passerby volunteered to be plasticuffed!

Perimeter patrol at Akuse Kpong farm's rice growing area. Watch out for bloody snakes, lads! The Bush is full of them. Team A of Course No. 5 makes its way warily out of the undergrowth.

The Volta Rover Authority Training School——spartan but functional where we had two classrooms with basic facilities.

Officers Course No.2. At the rear is Mr Lawson, Mr Quarshie & Mr Osei. Seated is Mr Miller sporting his UN medal for service with the Ghana Battalion in the Gaza Strip.

Relax guys, it's all over! Note Mr Mensah's national and UN medals. He is a real credit to his company.

Instruction on perimeter security (left), and a proud moment for my guards!

The children who joined in our pig roast can just be seen in the left of the picture. I found that I could not always eat in public if others had nothing. Alex Wysoki (in the white T-shirt), Gershwin Senior and friends devoured the pig or what was left of it after we decided to feed the children and not ourselves. If I remember correctly, the meat was still a bit pink as we ate it, but what the hell—normal rules didn't apply!

The final night at the clubhouse in Akuse. No-one had any money, nobody cared; we had a great time with the company of all who could make it, and the common language of friendship prevailed.

My farewell to my closest friends, the fire team at Akuse.
They had looked after me for a year and we had become great friends.
They asked for nothing, they were brave and a credit to the VRA and
their country.

HOLIDAY AND A RAPE

The time had come for my first break after six months of my contract. It was difficult to take on board that I was going to be exposed to normal things again like telephones, TV and unlimited food. The day before my flight it was a drive to Accra and the Dutch Agents' transit house near the airport. By the time I arrived I was too tired to visit the dubious pleasures of the city and crashed out ready for my trip the following morning. Due to the retention of my passport by the immigration authorities on my first arrival, this had to be obtained with the help of a VRA representative to whom I promised some special perfume for his latest girlfriend. Having got my passport, I made my way to the airport where I was whisked through the various controls, liberally handing out dash to speed up the required stamps. Finally, there it was, a British Caledonian Boeing sitting on the tarmac. It was enough to persuade me to become a 'Jock'. Before setting out on my journey I had experienced pain in my left eye and it became noticeably redder as time went on. By the time I had reached the aircraft it looked as if I had been whacked. The last Ghanaian at the top of the boarding steps took one look at me and said, "Don't worry, it's only Apollo Eye." He told me that anyone in Ghana who had witnessed the path of the Apollo spacecraft would suffer from the same complaint. However, the Chief Stewardess said it was the worse case of conjunctivitis she had ever seen. I was given some eye drops and advised to go straight to the Gatwick Medical Centre on arrival.

So there I was, home in the UK looking the worse for wear and two stone lighter in weight. My friend and colleague Michael Elliot picked me up at Gatwick and said I looked like shit and drove me to the nearest eating place he could find and I had a full fry English breakfast followed by a small cigar—and the last thing I remember before falling asleep in his 4x4 was that everyone was running even though they thought they were walking.

My family was in good shape as always, thanks to my wife. One of my sisters, Shirley, said, "Well, how is the black sheep of the family?" It felt odd being at home, looking at butcher's shops particularly, with so much to each and such a selection. In no small way it made me feel embarrassed that I now had so much and those I was working with had so little. Not being as helpless and innocent (which I found to my cost) as on my first trip out, I planned my return trip with the most useful things that I knew would help see me through.

The time came quickly enough for the return to the white man's grave, as everyone kept reminding me. There were certainly doubts in my mind. The lack of medical back-up, the absence of telephones, shortage of food and a dozen other reasons why a sane individual should not return to a place which God appeared to have neglected. But there was always the money, a prime factor when assessing the threat, and also the glimmer of interest for me personally. In Africa, the people, the need to make a mark—and I had not seen the breasts of the Methodist leader's eldest yet! I did a final assessment in the departure bar at Gatwick and after three large Bells the world seemed a better place. I ensured that I purchased 2 litres of the liquor of life and wrapped the bottles carefully in my hand luggage. I would not be seeing much whisky after these two bottles. Good whisky was hard to come by.

The flight started routinely and I settled down to the usual accompaniment of music, screams and continual movement of my fellow travellers. The best announcement I have ever heard on an aircraft was a personal request from the Captain that whoever had stolen the last toilet roll from the ladies' loo should return it or we would be forced to use the travel instructions booklet. It was at the time that the worst happened: there was a minor fault with our aircraft and the Captain informed us that we were en route to Kano in Nigeria to have it checked out. I noticed immediately that this did not go down well with the Ghanaian travellers and there was a hubbub of noise and disturbance and children began to cry and I was totally confused. After some time I managed to speak to a stewardess who informed me that there was a lot of ill feeling between Nigeria and Ghana, due to the Nigerians objecting to illegal immigrant labour from Ghana working in Nigerian mines and the petroleum and chemical industry, thereby depriving Nigerians of jobs. Nigeria was trying to implement forced repatriation of Ghanaians and my fellow travellers felt that they would be unwelcome at Kano and feared for their lives and property. This certainly put me on edge, not knowing anything about Nigeria or its people, and we had absolutely nothing in common which puts one at a disadvantage. This situation remained until we landed at Kano and then there was deathly silence as we awaited our next move. We were asked to disembark and were driven to the arrivals lounge, which was pretty awful, and with limited facilities. The lighting was poor and the toilets had seen better days. There was also some catcalling from green uniformed individuals with AK47s who looked as if they were on another planet. I began to become apprehensive when a small, ugly official said that the airport was now closed and that we would have to wait in the outside lounge. This proved to be roofed areas with benches outside facing the airport perimeter.

I could see that this was going to be a cold uncomfortable night with no means of refreshment or toilet facilities. It was easy for me to find a corner and use my hand luggage for a pillow. I had a pullover and this was enough to keep me warm. My fellow travellers were not so easily settled and the children were crying again and everyone was most miserable. I broke open one of my priceless whisky bottles and had a snort or two and then tried to make the most of it. I was awakened by screams coming from the garden area to my left where the frangipani trees were blooming. I looked to my nearest fellow traveller and asked what was going on. He whispered: "Soldiers have a girl." I didn't know what to do. I couldn't see them for the vegetation, but the noises were evidence enough. I looked for any policeman or anyone in authority, but there were none. I found my torch in my hand luggage and decided to try to intervene, though this could have been a mistake in many ways. The girl was pinned down on the ground and a soldier was having his way with her. Two others held her arms and two more already had their trousers at half-mast around their ankles. I saw that these guys were those earlier that had been catcalling. I shouted at them and said what the bloody hell was going on? The man on top of the girl stood up, showing his large member and I remember saying to him, "Is that all you've got or have your friends got bigger ones?" This seemed to give vent to some conversation; one of those with his pants down ran away and the other argued with the first that it was his turn. Then came the cavalry. If a Rhino has ever charged you, I'm sure this was similar. Four huge Ghanaian mamas, each weighing approximately 18 stone, literally ran them down and beat the crap out of them. Some other bright soul had also activated the fire alarm and a few lights came on. This was enough for the brave airport guards who had fled the field, bloodied but not dead. When some order had been restored I was fêted by the ladies and promised the earth when we arrived in Accra. The young girl was not badly hurt and was taken into the fold of her family. I did not realise what long ranging effect this would have on my time remaining in Ghana. Come daylight, the police went through the motions of statements, complaints and quickly ushered us back onto our aircraft during mid-morning. The rest of the flight was uneventful as everyone was exhausted. It was difficult to disengage myself from the rest of my fellow travellers at Accra Airport. We parted as blood brothers. Some three days later back in Akuse, Mr Nyametie sidled up to me.

"Bishop," he said, "you were sent from God to help protect us."

"How do you know that?" I enquired.

"Jungle Drums!" he smiled.

THE CHAPEL IN THE BUSH

On Sundays time hung heavy on my hands and when I found myself talking to the mirror I knew I had to do something or go bush crazy or try the local brew, which helped towards madness. I had seen how religious my friends were and decided it would be useful to join in their Sunday activities if I could find the right church. The earliest Christian missions in West Africa were Roman Catholic, introduced by the Portuguese. In Ghana, previously known as the old Gold Coast, the Basel Missionary Society began work in 1827 amongst the Ewe people. The Wesleyans who founded a mission in Kumasi in the Volta area followed these and the Fenti were the first to embrace Christianity. As time went on, a variety of religious factions had a profound influence on the evolution of the political geography of West Africa and sought to modify local customs, introducing in many areas new crops and implements, or even, in one case, bringing about improvements in local warfare techniques. The missions played a great part in the abolition of the slave trade which flourished here in the 17th and 18th centuries when thousands of West Africans were transported to the Americas, supplied in the main by fellow West Africans for gain. It was with all this in mind that I decided to further integrate with my neighbours by joining a church, even if for nothing other than to relieve the isolation on a Sunday. This was to be a major success.

I had had some training in the Methodist Church as a boy in a chapel in High Halden near Ashford, Kent. Being the children of a local farmer, my mother found that the Methodist minister was also the shopkeeper and that if we became part of his flock we would be favoured with bread, paraffin for our lamps and other essentials—so I became a Methodist. It was ironic that later in life I found that our minister had been sentenced for fraud for colouring grey paraffin pink and selling it at the higher price—so much for the men of the cloth.

It seemed to me that as you travelled from one village to another, there was a different religion in each place. I assumed it was down to whichever missionary got there first. For whatever reason, I carry a small Bible with me on my travels; not that I'm a Bible puncher, but it has got me out of one or two difficult spots when it was seen. I found there was a Methodist chapel in Akuse and decided to attend it on the next Sunday. First I had to find the right man to introduce me. Mr Nanka Bruce was a senior man in the VRA and I let slip that I wanted to go to church and then let it all happen. I found that the chapel had only a portion of a roof and only three walls were bricked in. There were some chairs and benches and a square altar. I drove down to the chapel on Sunday morning and to my surprise everyone was lined up to greet me—the Minister, the Committee and the local Chief. I was led into the building like a celebrity and felt a bit overawed, but kept up the role they obviously wanted me to play. I found I had been given the best chair to the right of the altar, facing the congregation sitting next to the chief. The men sat on one side of the church and the ladies sat on the other, being divided by the aisle. I was lucky because by dint of my previous time in High Halden Methodist choir I knew most of the hymns by heart. Everyone prayed with great dignity and hearty Amens. The first hymn was then sung with a small group making the music in lieu of organ, and they were good. As I knew the hymn, I decided to go for it and let go with gusto. To my amazement everyone began to dance. It didn't end there. We then formed a crocodile behind the chief and danced and weaved our way around the chapel, dancing in step with rhythm and hand clapping. As we passed the front of the altar there was an offering bowl into which we threw money—an African variation of the standard collection we know at home. The large African matrons who rule all were now smiling at me and I began to feel I was next on the menu. The quality of their village choir singing will remain with me always.

The chapel now had a special meaning for me and I was determined to make sure the roof and the walls were completed to make it weatherproof. We bought timber and local made bricks and within four weeks it looked good. A sign made in Accra added the right touch to the door and a party was held to celebrate the commissioning of the completed building. Additionally, the chapel elders from God-knows-where had produced purple robes, which were to be blessed at the ceremony. The whole Methodist community turned out in their best clothes, the young girls putting ash from the fires onto their faces to make them 'light skinned'. The singing was great and the ladies had dressed in white T-shirts and showed more breasts per metre than the M25. The men failed miserably with a mixture of old suits and bits and pieces. The collection exceeded any other and at the end of the day I knew I was at ease and at home with my neighbours. Before leaving I accepted an invitation from the chief to attend his village at Somania the following weekend for a party. This I will describe later.

The firm beliefs of my fellow Methodists convinced me that in Africa you are nearer to God. Their hunger, pain from illness and lack of all things, which we take for granted, was helped by their prayers and their regular church attendance. I noticed that they gazed enviously at my Methodist hymn book which I had found in Ashford, which also contained the music to the hymns and psalms in it. I decided to donate the book on my last week in Africa, suitably annotated for use in 'our' chapel. This was well received and I had to embrace the whole congregation. Paddy remarked to me that if we could fill a ship full of hymn books we could make an enormous profit in Ghana. I am seriously considering a further visit to my chapel to see if it is still standing and whether it could do with some repairs.

VISITORS

Visitors were a rarity. No one came to our isolated venue, but special mention must be made of two visitors. The first was the half yearly visit by a representative of our UK employers, a young man in his early thirties who was a whizz kid in all matters electronic, and he had a particular responsibility for finalising the physical security requirements in support of the manned guarding force which was our function. It was decided that he would spend his first day with the agent in Accra and then be picked up by me and brought to Akuse where he would be based whilst he conducted his surveys. He was duly collected from the agent's office and deposited at my bungalow. He was a nice enough guy who had obviously spent too much time in offices rather than out in the field. He was pale and a little unsure of Africa, which I could understand.

He spent the day travelling around the sites making his notes and then came back to the bungalow later in the day. It was suggested that we had something to eat and then take him out and show him the real Africa. Poor sod, I had hardly got accustomed to Africa and I wondered how he would cope with this unknown land. Off we went to Somania. The Accra agent who, with Paddy, had this perverse idea that this young man should be exposed to the local life, had now joined us. I still cannot think what it would have proved, except to place him at risk if he was of a nervous disposition.

We found our way to Somania to a small social club that had separate rooms if you wanted to stay over. It was typically spartan and used mostly by the locals for weddings and other parties. The landlady was a large charming woman who was pleased to see white men using her place. We had large bottles of beer sitting in her enclosed garden and the waitress was obviously one of her daughters who was wearing only a single dress and no underclothing. Our young man from the UK just stared and said nothing. The beer continued flowing but I could not settle and enjoy mine as I could see Paddy and his chum were cooking up a surprise for our guest and, for once, I did not think it appropriate.

I made my excuses and decided to go back to the bungalow. I was not happy with my borrowed old Peugeot 405 whilst my Nissan truck was being 'serviced'. There had been some funny noises from the front nearside that made me nervous as the last place you would want to be was stranded in the bush. I told the guys I would see them later if I was still awake. My two colleagues were still nudging each other and were obviously ready to set our visitor up for some joke or other. I left with some worry in my mind because our visitor did not know where he was; indeed, he might have been on another planet.

I had only been driving in the soft sandy track towards Akuse for about ten minutes when a grinding noise came from the front nearside wheel area and the car tipped in that direction and brought me to a halt. Fortunately I had only been driving at about 10 mph as it was deep sand and I had already taken my foot off the accelerator. I got out, but it was so damned dark I couldn't see a thing. My emergency box was still in the Nissan so I had nothing except what I stood up in. The tools from the car had long since been "borrowed" and I blamed myself for this oversight and leaned against the bonnet feeling that it was down in the wheel area—but there was nothing there! Somewhere I had lost the entire nearside front wheel and, gathering my thoughts, I had one slim chance that Paddy and the other guys would return by this track, although there were a number you could pick from. Alternatively, I could lock myself in the car and wait for daylight. There would be some traffic and I could take a chance and walk the 15kms to Akuse. None of these options seemed a good idea.

As I mulled it over I heard a twig snap on the other side of the car and the noise of something moving through the bush. I don't mind admitting I was scared. Was it a bloody great snake, or some other predator, looking for its supper? Whatever it was, it crossed the track and went back into the bush and I moved behind the car as it moved, keeping the car between myself and 'it'. As I gathered myself again, I was in for another shock as a voice said, "Good evening, how are you?" I swear I nearly came out of my clothing with fright. There, standing quite close to me, were three sets of white teeth in the darkness. Three hunters carrying muzzle-loading shotguns had seen the car lights stop.

I could not speak quickly enough to tell them I had lost a wheel and that I needed help. It never crossed my mind that they could have robbed and killed me on the spot. To my amazement these kind and helpful men actually found three of the wheel nuts in the sand, and between us we got the wheel back on. In the light of the car headlights I could now see more of their ancient muzzle loading guns. They reminded me of the boat punt guns used for duck shooting on our lakes in the last century. These hunters used match heads to explode their charge. I gave them all the local money I had, the equivalent of five pounds sterling, and they were grateful. I also said that I would leave some large boxes of red English matches at Alice's roadside beer shop for their collection. They said they had to go to catch the early morning antelope as they grazed near the lake. I was never to meet these unknown men again but they were indeed Samaritans.

I completed my journey without further incident and had to be satisfied with a cup of tea before bed. I was awoken to the noise of two drunken men banging on the bedroom window announcing with glee that they had gone through the pretext of bedding down in Somania and then, when their young visitor was asleep, they had legged it, abandoning him to his own mercies! I was not too amused at their joke and knew it would be dawn soon and with a dodgy car I could not recover the guy until daylight. I must have slept until after 8am, waking with a start and thinking, bloody hell, I wonder how that poor sod got on when he found himself alone? I dressed and checked my car wheels, tightened the offending wheel nuts to make sure that they would cope and set off for Somania.

Paddy and the agent were still out cold in their bungalow. The drive was smooth and the morning still fairly cool. Children waved and smiled as I entered the village and it was not too difficult to find the rest house. I parked up on the hard sand outside and entered, not knowing what I would find. There he was, sitting at a table with the lady of the house having coffee with the young girl holding his hand. "Hi Roy, how are you?" he asked. "Where are the other guys—have they got a problem?" I shook my head, "No, I thought I would collect you for breakfast. I still have two tins of beans and some eggs." He said his goodbyes to the ladies and I was sure the mum was eyeing him as a prospective son-in-law. He promised to return in four months and even wrote down their shoe sizes to bring gifts next time.

As we got into the car he didn't seem to have a care in the world. After falling asleep he had no idea he was alone and knew nothing until he was awoken by the young lady bringing him some coffee and a bowl of hot water. He didn't say any more, just sat and hummed some tuneless music until we reached the bungalows. Paddy and the agent were just stirring and he spotted them. "Great night, guys, thanks very much. There was a bill for 40,000 Cedis which I told them you would settle up today. Best night's sleep I've had for awhile—see you later." I could see Paddy and the agent looking at each other. Maybe their prank had misfired?

He showered whilst I heated up the beans, boiled four eggs and made some toast. When he came out of the shower there was the evidence, love bites and other signs of affection on his pale body. Our young visitor had had an experience he would never forget and it was all due to the misguided intentions of his 'friends'. The agent drove him back to Accra after his short stay. He really didn't want to leave but that was understandable!

So much for the UK visitor. Our next visitors, surprisingly, were a group of American students who were touring West Africa as part of their studies. The overland bus-type vehicle they arrived in contained their sleeping accommodation, feeding, toilet and shower facilities and the vehicle looked like a spacecraft. God knows what my gentle Ghanaians thought as it pulled up in a cloud of dust outside the training school lecture rooms. There were about twelve visitors, eight white and four black Americans. The whites alighted fairly quickly and wanted to stretch their legs and take the air, which in fact, was blistering in the nearly afternoon. Oddly, the black students did not leave the vehicle.

The Americans didn't know how to handle their visit and I think they thought we were all sub-humans and certainly not on their planet. They actually talked to us as if we were children with comments like, "Gee, how can you live in a place like this?" and, "How do you contact the outside world?" We explained: "Oh, we drive 100kms to reach any normal facilities." Then the next question: "What do you do for fun?" and we replied: "We go fishing and go to church." They shook their heads. To their credit, some delved in the bus and handed out sweets, chewing gum and some magazines. My students did not say much and just kept looking at this strange party.

I was invited to climb on board the bus to admire the facilities that included a video and TV screens everywhere. The bus also had air conditioning and an ice-cream machine and the ever-popular Coca Cola machine. It was a home from home. I met the black students and asked them if they wanted to look over the training school. They were not interested and I asked them if they wanted to chat to my guys, but again no interest was shown. They were subdued for some reason. After an hour the bus set off for Akasombo to see the dam. The farewells were genuine enough but the net result was that we were worlds apart. I asked Mr Boateng what he thought about the Americans. He mused for a while and said, "They have too much—they have forgotten how to live. Those black men are not Africans, they play with the name." This was a subject I didn't press any further.

THE FRIGHTENED GIRL

Returning to the bungalow late one evening I parked the pickup under the canopy and went to unlock the outer porch door. I found it open with a piece of paper attached to the lock. The light switch was inside the bungalow so I unlocked the front door, put on the lights and read the note from Kingsley: "A girl needs your help, Mr Bishop. She is without friends and has come to seek assistance." What girl, I thought—and there she was, huddled up on the floor in the corner of the porch. It had been so dark I could not see her. She looked at me with wide eyes. She was about 12 years old and still a child.

"What do you want, young lady?" I asked. I had to keep this absolutely right as my neighbours were viewing the porch and they obviously knew the girl was there. "What do you do?" I brought her a chair and thought it best not to take her inside, as I wanted witnesses.

Her English was perfect, as with all the children.

"I have been given away," she said, and I thought she meant in marriage, as it was customary to do so with no real hang-ups in the village.

I think the rule was that if you had a number of wives you had to maintain them comfortably. However, this was not the case. She had been given to the local medicine man—we know them as the witchdoctors—as repayment for a debt of her uncle. Bloody hell, what do we do now? I was aware that what we know as black magic and other names, voodoo and spirit worship, was practiced in my patch, but I had decided not to touch on the subject or explore the matter in any way. I had seen some items hanging on the pathway to a fishing village but had been assured they were for good luck. I pondered on the fact that a lot of the things I learnt about had been customs for thousands of years and how does one change a complete culture? The very darkest of black magic was the sacrificial killing of children and the selling of their body parts for the making of spells for enhanced sexual power and, in even worse cases, the destruction of another person. I knew there was the use of body parts, as when I visited the cemetery in Accra to look at the military section in an old corner area, the graves had been desecrated and, sadly, the graves of some children had been opened shortly after burial. This confirmed that there was a market in voodoo charms.

Previously, in the corner where my front path joined the porch, I had seen an upturned earthenware pot which I thought might look good on an inside windowsill. As I was going to get it, having mentioned it to Kingsley, he shot after me shouting, "No, no, it is Ju Ju!" I found that everyone except myself knew that the pot contained a spirit, a Ju Ju, and it should not be disturbed or bad luck may follow. I never did move that pot. When in Rome, do as the Romans do. It shows that even a Jehovah's Witness has two beliefs—funny old world, isn't it?

There was now a small gathering outside my residence including the white wife of an engineer who wanted to take the child into her home, but this was not going down too well with my Ghanaian colleagues. They did not want to be involved and their every other phrase was, "This is a family matter." Her village was about 12 miles away and it was late. We made a bed for the girl on the porch, made some food for her and I gave the last of my cola tins. I was told that her parents would come to collect her in the morning. Fortunately it was a Saturday and I would be in for a while. I eventually fell asleep a much troubled man.

Sure enough, in the morning I peered out through my lattice style window and there, standing in the road, were two men and two women. The women were dressed colourfully as usual. One man was obviously a farmer, and the other I immediately took a disliking to. He wore a long cloak and some form of head-dress, which was turban-like. He also had many things hanging around his neck. The girl made no effort to join them and had waited for me.

I wondered whether this was going to be my first real confrontation and how it would go. Then two of my friends arrived—Mr Nyameti, the fire chief, and Mr Boateng, my fishing adviser. These two characters I trusted.

"What can I do?" I asked. "I cannot let this child be given away although I know it is the custom; but she came to me for help and that means it is my problem."

One said to me, "Your biggest problem is that you are a white man. If you were the spiritualist you would be doing what he is doing. She will cook for him, work in the fields for him and warm his bed at night. Can you see anything wrong in that?"

For a moment I could not disagree. "What shall I do, guys? We all need to come out of this looking good."

They both smiled.

Negotiate Roy—let's have a meeting. So there we were in my living room discussing the life of a young girl curled up on my spare mattress on the porch. I made tea, making sure that the spiritualist was served first and that the ladies had theirs in the kitchen, being looked after by a bemused Kingsley. Thank God English was the national language.

I played the innocent white man and let my two friends blame my lack of knowledge for the benefit of my visitors. Soon I could see they were feeling comfortable and then came the question. Would I take on the debt of the family? I quickly thought about it—surely it cannot be too much. What happens if I do? Will I have a queue of helpless ones coming to me for help?

"What is the debt?" I asked.

It was five sacks of maize corn and rent on land set aside for the crop that failed. We settled for two sacks of rice, a crate of 24 tins of Canadian lager and 100,000 Cedis (about £25). I sent Kingsley to the rice farm and he was back in less than 15 minutes. I, in the meantime, had scrounged the crate of beer off Alex Wysocki, my Canadian friend, and had the cash in my security box. This was handed over with ceremony outside my bungalow. The parting did not quite take place then as I found they had no means of transportation. We then went off in my pickup to Atwa, twelve miles away, where there was another great show of the spiritualist doing his thing and ordering his other wives to unload and carry in the goodies. The girl's father grovelled on the ground, showing his devotion, the two ladies singing his praises. I shook hands around, showing respect for this man I did not respect. I went to get into the pickup and there was the young girl. We had not talked much and she held out her hand and said, "Thank you. My name is Mary."

On return to Akuse I did not know what to expect, but there was not a ripple on the water. When I saw Kingsley I asked him what his good book says about this event. I do not know whether this event was linked to the finding of corn maize on my doorstep at least once every week and four corns on the cob, which were welcome. I never found out who kindly left them for me.

When is kindness interpreted as weakness? Do we have the right to interfere with local affairs? As always, it was smile, and soak up the results.

THE PIG

Alex Wysocki, the Canadian trouble-shooting engineer, was one of the few white neighbours in our township. He and his wife Barbara came from Essex and were a kind couple, devoting much of their time to supporting the local VRA employees and their families. Their door was always open to people in trouble, but in some cases their kindness was their worst enemy as just about everyone tried to take advantage of their hospitality. Fred, their driver and handyman, who would have made most athletes in the European circuit go green with envy, protected them. He ran like the wind, played football like a superstar, but was not interested in the invitation to go to Europe for a soccer test. He was content where he was and he had also just found a new girlfriend called Patience.

Alex suggested that he have a pig roast and barbecue style event in the grounds of the old Italian social club. We thought this was a great idea as most of the time we were hungry for decent meat. "Where the hell do you find a pig?" I asked, but he knew of a farmer near Somania who kept pigs and they were reputed to be disease free and good for 'chop' (eating). We drove to Somania to view the animal and there, down a dusty track inside a fenced enclosure, was a herd of pigs. They were whites and from my farming background they were the biggest pigs I had seen and were clean and seemed to be fed on roots from a variety of trees and bushes. The pig farmer was beside himself with joy at the thought of being able to sell one of his stocks for a good profit and this involved considerable haggling, but we finally settled on three sacks of rice, 200,000 Cedis (about £25), three crates of Canadian beers and a digital watch I had kept hidden for such emergency moments! We secured the agreement and all that was left now was to plan the day, the killing and the cooking of our selected giant pig.

A Saturday afternoon was selected and Alex planned to visit the Canadian High Commission to get more beers and, if we were lucky, maybe there was even a bottle of whisky though generally it was not available. Still, the beers would do. We invited our closest friends and colleagues from the Volta River Authority and in the end it turned out to be a bit of an open house with the best laid plans going awry. The idea was to kill the pig on the Friday afternoon, hand it up to drain overnight and commence roasting it the following morning. I was not too keen on being there for the killing, but we needed at least five men to lift the pig into the back of the pickup truck. Alex hand-made two lassos—one for him and one for me, the idea being that we would lasso the pig's head and take the strain on either side of the animal to hold it still while the farmer cut its throat. Things did not go according to plan as we positioned the lassos, but as soon as we took the strain the pig took off like a tank. It went through the wattle fencing, dragging Alex and I behind it and we had to hold on because if it got away and went into the bush I don't know when we would find it. We were covered in pig shit and mud and cut by splinters from the fence. I managed to regain my footing and noticed that Alex's silver hair and beard had turned a nasty brown and he was not enjoying it. Round the trees we went until we came to a narrow path and looped the ropes around two coconut palms. This brought the pig to a halt, but it was immensely strong and I thought it would uproot the trees; but the farmer was quick—a swift stroke and the porker was dead. Alex and I formed a firmer friendship that day and it took a lot of beer to take away the aches and pains. A round of applause greeted us as we dragged the pig to the truck with just about every child in the district wanting to assist.

Back to Akuse we went with our prize where we hung the beast half in and half out of the pickup. The next step was the disembowelling which I decided to pass on, although I had seen my grandfather do it on the farm. The pig's guts, liver and all its bits were the gift to the guards who would protect it until the morning. I am sure they fed well from these delicacies.

Alex and I decided to check the security of our pig during the night and he walked up to my bungalow at about three in the morning. I was not unconvinced that this time was too early as the pig was so important to us it warranted some extra attention. Rather than go straight across the old tarmac road to the clubhouse car park, he suggested we cut around through the bush and come up on the opposite side where there was a cleared field upon which the kids tried to play football with a ball of grass. We struggled a bit as there was no moon and it was difficult to find our way, but once we found the edge of the open area we started to cross—but I heard something move in front of us. It sounded like sandpaper being rubbed and we both had our large torches, which we had intended using, but this was unexpected. We switched on the lights and there was a huge snake with a partridge-type bird in its mouth that it had obviously just stalked. Alex and I were frozen—what the hell if its mate was around? We moved more quickly around this feeding reptile and legged it towards the club. Needless to say, our two guards were fully alert, having heard our shouts and seen our lights. "Snake!" I exclaimed. "A bloody big snake on the football field." The guards assured me not to worry but it took me a while to settle down, having seen the hungry snake. I am sure it would not attack a human unless it was a small and helpless baby, but I had heard that small goats and domestic fowl were the victims of large reptiles. The pig was still there; the fireplace was ready and I began to dream of that pork crackling, which I had not eaten for some months. Roll on the party feast!

Overnight Mr Miller, my assistant drill instructor, had erected a roasting spit and said he had got it from the Akosombo Stores Section. As usual, one did not ask questions. We lit a large charcoal fire in the pit and with a lot of shoving and heaving we got our pig on the spit and positioned across the fire. All we had to do now was turn it and, more importantly, make sure it did not disappear, as by now the word was out that there was food to be had. The pig roasted throughout the morning, being turned by a volunteer who seemed to be tasting the meat frequently. Around midday we assembled at the clubhouse and pooled our beer tins, Cokes and Seven-up bottles and there was a variety of refreshments from a variety of people. This was one of the few social occasions I was to experience. Looking back, we should have done it more often, but such is life. Small talk between the party players was about world politics, oddly enough. There was a lot of humour and Ghanaians have the ability to laugh at themselves, which is much like the English humour. It was a very relaxed scene. I did notice that there were not many ladies, but this did not deter Alex's wife and our Accra contacts lady helping out. The pig was reaching perfection and I noticed it was going to be a hairy pig—but our hunger pangs put paid to any worries in that field. We had some plates and a large tray of bread slices. There were tomatoes and onions mixed as a salad and a large bowl of water in which to wash our fingers. Music came from a battery driven ghetto blaster and most of the songs were by Willie Nelson and Joan Armatrading, followed by a bit of Wagner!

Alex and Gershwin carved slices from the pig and handed them out. There was silence and everyone stuffed down this tasty repast. It was heaven—I had forgotten how sweet pork was. The crackling was hairy indeed, but who cares—the hairs went down as well. There was a lot of lip smacking and contented noises from the thirty odd people present. As we queued for a second time around I became aware that we had an audience of about forty pairs of eyes staring at the pig and I suddenly felt embarrassed. We had been stuffing our faces whilst less fortunate ones stood by. I found that I could not eat my second helping whilst being watched. What to do? I sidled over to Alex who was also aware of our uninvited guests and he spread his hands. "Bish, do what you feel you should do—you know I will do the same." Gershwin was next to Alex and he knew that we were disturbed. He said, "Remember, this if Africa. Sometimes you cannot do everything and you must harden your heart." He was right, of course—this is how life was.

We soon reached a solution. All the guests had another generous second helping with myself doing overkill on the crackling. There was still a third of the pig left and it would have fed us for some time had we taken it home; but as you might guess, we gave it away. The children were lined up sitting on the ground and slowly and fairly we distributed the pork amongst them. Any adult with them had their share too. The pig refused to be beaten and there was still meat and bones left and, more importantly, the head. What to do with the head? Among the guests was a retired bank manager. He was about 70 years old, which was rare indeed for Ghana. I held him in great esteem and approached him for the advice on what to do with the remnants of the pig. He suggested that the pieces should be distributed amongst the invalid members of the village and the orphanage at Somania should have the huge head for their consumption. This was well thought out; there were enough bits and pieces to make a base for the soup or stew-like dish known as Ghana chop. We cut and boxed the leftovers of our pig and they were transported off to our selected residents. We poured beer onto the ground as a libation offering to the gods. All in all, this was a day not to be missed. Pork remains my favourite meat dish and I continue to have visions of our pig.

LEISURE TIME

There was never really any leisure time. One was always doing something for the project but you could combine business with pleasure, as they say. What do you do where there was no TV, radio or telephone? You could not even 'plane spot' as none passed in the sky overhead. It was isolation at its best.

There was the local beer—Star, it was called—bottled in litre size green bottles and it passed for a poor lager. All the roadside shacks sold beer and sometimes I saw it being cooled by lumps of ice—where the hell do you get ice from in the middle of nowhere?

As we worked until midday on Saturday there was not a lot of time left with just Sunday, and on that day I got into the routine of my chapel visit. I had brought my fishing rod with me to Ghana and as we were on the side of the largest lake in West Africa I decided to try and catch something. I was lucky to befriend Mr Boateng, a member of the small fire section in Akuse, who offered to help me catch a fish. I nicknamed him my fishing adviser and he took great pride in announcing this in the VRA township. As I was part of the good guys I was allowed to fish off the Kpong Dam near the training school. Normally this was out of bounds. Mr Boateng used to find worms and meet me at the side of the road approaches to the dam and we tried our luck. The lake teemed with a fish called Tilapia, perch like and indeed most edible. They seized the bait very much like a trout strikes. I tried fishing deeper on the bottom and one evening when the mozzies were humming around my head I made contact with an enormous catfish. I could not reel it in so we had to drag it sideways until we found a way to climb down to it. It made noises like a child crying—I was glad when it was put out of its misery. Mr Boateng was beside himself with joy, as he knew I would give it to him and that this large fish would supplement his food larder for a week. So regularly off we went, my fishing adviser and I, down to the lake and tried for a good catch for the Boateng family and friends.

In the lake there are Perch that grow to the size of a man and they make good eating. I knew a hunter who used to shoot them as they sunned themselves on the surface and he made a good living from the proceeds. There was one occasion when my fishing adviser could not accompany me to the Dam so I went along with Sarpong who sat in the truck trying to analyse the odd fishing actions of the white man. I knew that if he had a grenade he would have thrown it in the lake and collected the stunned fish. There was no finesse with Sarpong. He spoke his mind and operated on whatever basic instinct was the most prominent. He had been a bad boy in the past. I caught some Tilapia and small Perch and then decided to try my luck near the small boat jetty, which protruded out into the lake. I thought there might be eels there but I bore in mind that you did not know what you would catch. Before long my float dived away under the dark water, similar to a Tench bite in the UK. There was some pressure on the top section of my rod and I knew it was a heavy fish. I carefully reeled it in so that it lay on the sloping jetty so I could take a look at it. Sarpong came out of the cab of the truck like he had been stung. "Electric, Electric!" he howled. I found I had caught the one and only electric eel in my life. It was an ugly, fat thing with brown and green speckled skin and an ugly mouth. I stepped back a bit and cut my line, handing the loose end to Sarong who dragged it up onto the road near the truck. "No eat, no good eating," he went on, so I left it alone and went back to catching something that at least looked like a fish. When Sarpong drove me back to the bungalow I noticed that the electric eel was nowhere to be seen. The next day in the office I asked him what had happened to the electric fish? He smiled and said, "Good chop, I make babies last night." Whilst Sarpong might think this was an aphrodisiac, I noticed that Alfred and Emmanuel shook their heads. In their opinion Sarpong was not on this planet.

Another rather more unfortunate tale involving Sarpong came about during tea break one afternoon when the young telex operator stopped me and said there had been a big explosion in Accra and that people had been hurt. Unfortunately he had no other clarification of the details. Two hours later at the office we were just packing up for the day when we heard the screech of brakes outside and there was Sarpong who had been on a mail run to the city that day. I could see that he and the car were covered in brown mud lumps, some of which had gone in through the driver's window. Then we caught the smell of this mud that turned out to be excrement. "What has happened, Sarpong?" He was not happy; his face was covered in crap and so was the car. "The town sewage system has blown up," he explained and said he had just been passing the public toilets on the side of the main sewage treatment plant when the entire works blew up. Adjoining shacks were blown away and several people were hurt but the blast mercifully went upwards. Two men using the loo at the time were blown upwards and outwards over the main road; one had apparently tossed a lit match down the bog hole and the build up of methane gas exploded. The contents of the sewage plant now lay across the road on a sand and rock covered open area. Emmanual and Alfred saw Sarpong and called him Mr Shitman. They were both in stitches rolling around and killing themselves with laughter. Sarpong did not see the funny side of this and chased them down the road brandishing the car jack handle. Fortunately he failed to catch them. We helped him regain face with a fairly generous dash of money, which included the cost of car cleaning. Despite his efforts the next day the car still smelt strongly of manure and particularly when the engine was red-hot. Sarpong got his revenge on our two office wallahs some three months later—he brought them some vegetables to have with their lunch, of which they were very appreciative. After they had eaten Sarpong smiled maliciously and informed them he had bought them from a seller who grew them in the sewage! Apart from the sound of mouth washing there was silence.

In addition to my fishing trips and church on Sundays there was the monthly trip to Accra to replenish my food cupboard, collect mail from the Dutch Agent, draw some spending money and for a few hours try to pretend that life was near normal. Receiving the mail was an event. The letters would be six weeks old, which was the turnaround time for our communication with the UK. Thank God nothing too serious happened, as links with home were so poor. My mother sent me a copy of the *Kentish Express* every week to keep me up to date and this kept me fairly balanced. The regular arrival of my newspaper, just rolled up with some sellotape around it, never failed to cheer, especially since inside in addition to a letter was always a £10 note sterling. With £10 sterling a man could rule the world here. I shall be eternally grateful for this support from home. Letters could be stolen or go astray, but not an out-of-date newspaper. So, armed with my money and the latest news, I could then have a trip to Accra town to see the sights. There was not much to see as the roads were poor, the traffic lights did not work and there was a ramshackle air about everything. I saw a huge sign that read 'Supermarket'. I thought I could buy my supplies there, but when I went inside there was a family of goats living there. It was a sorry sight with empty broken shelves and signs that suggested this was once a thriving business.

The shops we bought our goods from were run in the main by Lebanese shopkeepers who had lived in Ghana for years. They had the very basics—tins of beans and peas, soap and washing materials, some wine and suspect spirits, cheap medical spirits and household items, but enough for me to stock up for the coming month. I changed my £10 note in the first shop and the owner gave me a small present of sweets for this transaction. I thought that the kids in Akuse would enjoy these. The next shopping stop was the Ghanaian fruit and vegetable lady near the airport. Here I could buy a form of lettuce, spring onions, pineapple and bananas, carrots and yams—enough for a while. Looking back, I suppose in the main I lived on tinned beans, fruit and fish, which is a fairly healthy diet. Then it was back to the Dutch Agent's guesthouse or to a hotel. Not quite like our hotels, but there was a bed, loo and a washbasin. We were fortunate on one visit when the Dutch agent took us out for supper. There were eight of us and in order to pay for the meal in the local currency of Cedis, he had to carry it in a plastic shopping bag such as you would normally get at home in the supermarket. It took ages to count out what was really a reasonable sum in sterling.

The Ghana Veterans Association was a watering hole in Accra, established just after the Second World War for those gallant Ghanaians who went off to do their bit and fought in North Africa and Europe. Their club building was built on the lines of an army mess that had seen better days, but was the home of people like Paddy and I. The service was on the lines of an officer's mess and the rules and staff acted out their roles as if we were at home in Aldershot—old habits are the best. We joined the Association for about £5 annual membership, which gave us another link to our host country. In fact, we only made about three visits as the training was demanding and Accra was 100kms away. One of the veterans I met was Oscar. Now in his eighties, Oscar had served with the Gold Coast Regiment from 1941 to 1948 and then with the 81st Division in Burma. He was the proud holder of the Burma Star medal. The Veterans Association, with help from a UK charity, had found a small house for Oscar and given him some financial support for living costs. Oscar was very proud of his time in the British Army and misses the comradeship.

Another friend in Accra came as a complete surprise. Who should be running the British Army Training Team (BATT) in Ghana than none other than Major Ian Chapman PARA who had been a good friend during my time in 6th Field Force in the UK—what a small world! Ian and his family kindly put me up for a weekend and I enjoyed real food, good wine and a visit to their club swimming pool. Ian and his family were fairly settled, but had to come to terms with the heat, snakes in his garden and the constant threat of illness. I know that his wife contracted some dreaded virus and was very ill, but thank God she recovered. Thank you, Ian, for that weekend as it helped me face my own problems better knowing that there was at least one point of refuge to run to if I needed help.

On one visit, after having done all our chores, we were invited to the downtown nightclub where all the Europeans went. Hell, it was just like the Wild West with loud music, beer going down like there was no tomorrow and squealing girls fighting over who was to have who. I saw that Paddy was boring the pants off two Germans who ran the sugar cane factory near Akuse. Both of them were drunk daily but they managed to produce sugar nonetheless. After a while they got tired of standing at the bar and found seats at a large table away from the dance area. I had been doing my best impression of jumping up and down dancing with a nubile young lady when I thought it was time to sit and have another tin of beer. I sat with the Germans, chatting about my time in their land, when I saw that Paddy was becoming agitated and moving about on his seat. I asked him if he was okay and he nodded and mopped his brow. The Germans were falling off their seats with laughter, which was odd for them, being normally not humorous. My German was good enough to understand that they had paid a young lady to crawl under the table and fondle Paddy's parts! Paddy was too embarrassed to run in case people thought he had arranged for this service. I let Paddy experience a little more pain or pleasure before I leaned under the table and grabbed the belt of her pants and pulled her off. Paddy adjusted his dress and legged it back to the bar. In the future days every time we passed the Germans on the road to Akuse they made gestures of an international nature, which never helped Paddy's blood pressure.

I noticed Paddy did not like the advances of the girls who were pretty, very young but old for their age. He kept himself aloof at the bar and tried to drink the place dry. All the beer was bottled with some tins of Canadian beer—it got stranger by the moment. The floorshow was a young lady dancing with a python snake, which left little to the imagination, and then two other ladies did an erotic dance, although actually I am not sure if they were ladies. Back to the dance floor and everyone having a great time, the music was good and the company was acceptable and it was not long before our driver took two well-pickled men back to our hotel. The next morning, inhaling deeply, I had a fruit juice breakfast and walked down the road to the guesthouse which was full of Dutchmen on tour where I hoped to get a real breakfast. It was quiet as I entered, but then I saw a naked girl sitting on the settee in the lounge painting her toenails. Maintaining my calm I asked where the guys were and she pointed to the first floor main bedroom. I went up the stairs, knocked on the door and got my next shock. There was my fellow Dutchman from last night buried under, I believe, three young girls and they were all sound asleep. I turned and did a runner to the kitchen where I found Helen the cook making coffee and complaining about these bad girls invading her place. Eventually everybody appeared and the young ladies left in a taxi and some order was restored. Everyone agreed it had been a good party.

It was then back to Akuse stopping on the way at a friendly beer shack to have a hair of the dog and sit and talk about life with the villagers who knew us well by now. We were accepted and that made life good. When we arrived at Akuse the water was not flowing and we could not have a shower. Never mind, there was always tomorrow. Perhaps the swimming pool had water in it. There was a neat handwritten note pushed under the door inviting us to a gathering at the provincial chief's residence the following weekend, which was something out of the norm. So that is how I spent my few leisure hours—fishing, praying, shopping, and the odd night out in Accra.

Whilst in Accra on one Saturday we were in the agent's office sorting out our mail and sending telex reports to the UK when the Dutch agent said: "Do us a favour Roy, could you give a lift to Elizabeth back to the customs office at the airport? She has been very helpful by authorising a number of import licences." I went into the next office and there sat an attractive customs officer who was obviously in a good mood. "Okay, no problem. It will only take a few minutes." I said hello to Elizabeth and said this way for your taxi and led her down the stairs.

I could hear some laughing as we went out to the car park and I noticed that my so-called friends were waving from the first floor windows. We had not gone more than twenty yards when Elizabeth put her hand on my thigh and whispered, "Have you something for me?" With difficulty I managed to reach the airport car with the customs officer's hand inside my trousers, steering with one hand and fighting off this fairly serious young woman who obviously had been down this route before. I stalled the pickup, as I could not change gear. As we kangarooed to a halt I reached into my shopping bag for anything I could find. She let go and alighted from the truck with a bottle of cheap wine and a pineapple and I was free. When I got back to the office I found I had been set up and most of the erratic driving had been seen through binoculars. Apparently this was a routine part of one's welcome to the club. Needless to say, I was not the only victim of Elizabeth, as I howled with laughter when an electronic systems guy from the UK was afforded the same experience and actually got out of his vehicle and hid behind the trees at the airport entrance until the lady got bored and walked the rest of the way.

The ultimate was the visit of a German sales executive who was fairly and squarely caught by Elizabeth. He was seen to be busily engaged in the front seat of the company Landrover. Witnessed by his so called friend, his contract was agreed.

THE DRUMS

Since I saw my first Tarzan film at the cinema I was aware of the jungle drums. I had heard them in about every African movie that was produced; did these instruments of music and communication really exist? I have heard many a person refer to the drum information system even whilst in the army where I likened their sounds to that of the Morse Code I was taught as a signaller on my radio-training course at Chichester. Maybe there's little difference—there has to be a common alphabet in order for one to understand the communication.

One day I was standing on top of the Akosombo Dam, one side looking outwards towards the north with its huge expanse of water that in the main was fairly calm, the south side giving way to the massive drop down the face of the dam to where the water exited after passing through the hydro electric generation system and then on down the River Volta until the next dam at Kpong near Akuse where the water levels were not so far apart. Where the water existed from the Akosombo Dam from within the bowls of that huge concrete giant, stunned and helpless fish came to the surface, having had more than a bumpy ride from the lake to the river below. These huge fish were fair game for the riverside fishermen who found it an easy way of getting a good catch instead of netting, line fishing or trying to harpoon basking perch. On this occasion I heard the most terrible screams down at the foot at river level and there was a fisherman spinning in his wooden canoe, round and round as he was sucked into a whirlpool-like waterhole created by the force of the water on its way outwards. His fellow fishermen were shouting and closing in as near as they dared, but they were reluctant to touch the edge of the swirling water. It was not long and he was gone. The canoe surfaced shortly afterwards about 600 metres down river but of the unfortunate man there was no sign. His friends crisscrossed the river but to no avail—he was lost. The dam management had witnessed this incident from their lofty control post but they too were as helpless as we were. The Chief Executive happened to be visiting that day which in some ways was opportune. To my amazement I heard him instruct the Chief Engineer to tell the fishermen to leave the base of the dam and move their canoes back out of danger. He had some authority in this matter, as the VRA owned the land upon which their village stood, and I think they enjoyed some support in return for the interference in their life, an agreement made before the dam construction was started. I thought, how is he going to speak to them as there are no telephones or radios? Is someone going to find his or her way to the village and see the Chief? It came as a complete surprise when I heard the drums beating out the Chief Executive's instructions. It sounded a bit like an old train travelling at speed—*clickety clack, clickety clack*—but it was a good base noise. It was amazing how those drum noises travelled several miles, particularly over water. It wasn't long before, sure enough, there was a move by all of the canoes away from the dam and they stood off at about 500 metres and recommenced fishing.

Some weeks later I made a point to get Mr Boateng to guide me to the fishing village as my curiosity had got the better of me. I wanted to see the drums. Making sure I had got some sweets for the kids and some bottles of beer for the Chief, we found our way over rough tracks. These, I realised, the fisher folk did not need to travel—or by road—for they had the river which was much smoother and easier to travel downstream, though bloody hard work on the way back when you have to use a paddle. As we entered the village I saw one of my first cows. It was tethered to a large tree. I turned up at the wrong time as I witnessed two men kill it with an axe-type weapon and they did not make a very good job of it.

"Bloody hell, Mr Boateng, what do they want to do that for?"

Mr Boateng looked at me as if I was suffering a touch of bush madness. "It's for chop (eating). Too much fish makes a man infertile."

I wondered if I should believe everything Mr Boateng says.

We drove slowly into the village as the kids and chickens were trying to commit suicide under the wheels of the truck. Mr Boateng was giving regal waves whilst I tried to find a place to stop, as by now we had so many interested people pressing to shake hands and say welcome. There, outside the Chief's residence, a bungalow of half homemade brick and timber, and under a canopy, were the drums. Not much to look at—a hollowed tree trunk, which looked as if it were several hundred years old, and four different size drumsticks propped up against the log. There were two wooden stools which suggested it could be a double act.

The top of the drum trunk had been planed into three thicknesses from which I assumed came the different notes. The Chief was a pleasant man, extremely well educated. He told me his son was nursing in the UK on a one-year contract and was very much missed. I could see that life in the village was peaceful with everyone just getting on with living as best they could. It appeared that their fish was taken daily to Accra for sale in the main markets from which they enjoyed a return that was good enough for the village welfare. I gave the Chief my dozen bottles of beer and also the kids' sweets, which in turn was given to his wife to tour the village giving the kids handouts. We passed the time of day; it was somewhere where you could lose yourself with only the noise of the children and the river as it passed.

Mr Boateng suddenly leaned over to me and whispered: "Time to go, Mr Bishop, I do not want you to be embarrassed." I took his advice and with much ceremony paid our farewells to the Chief. The children sang a song, everyone applauded and slowly off we went to find our way to the main road. "What was my problem, Mr Boateng?" I asked. He started laughing, obviously having his own private joke. "Come on, Mr Boateng, what was going to happen?" He said: "Soon you would have to eat monkey! It is a great honour as there are not many monkeys left." And off he went again into peels of laughter. I countered this joke on myself by saying, "In Singapore I ate snake and lizard and I was fine." He was quiet for a while and then said with great seriousness: "Africans do not eat lizards, only the Chinese." Moments like this I am sure the reader would agree are priceless. So there you have it. The drums do exist. They do work and I was to hear them again—once announcing the death of the Director of Communications following a traffic accident, and the other announcing the birth of a director's first son. It would be interesting to understand the vocabulary used by the drummers.

When we returned to my bungalow, Kingsley was still there. A young lady who rejoiced under the name of Betty Tete was standing by him. Against Kingsley's approval I allowed Betty to enter our bungalow and have tea. Kingsley went off in a huff and Betty stayed for tea and chatted about her impoverished state. When she left she took with her 20,000 Cedis, two cooking saucepans and, I suspect, my only pair of scissors.

A TRIP TO THE SEASIDE

We had a three-day break from the training programme to celebrate a local public holiday. Three days in Akuse would test the patience of even the hardiest white man. We planned a fishing trip, a visit to the once stately home of an earlier colonial governor at Suhum (where the hill wind was known affectionately as "London breeze") and a trip to the seaside at Prampram.

Four of us crammed into Alex Wysocki's 4x4 and we set off to the coast some 100kms to the south. The road, as always, was badly potholed and we could never drive in a straight line as you tried to miss the worst bumps, which probably added another 5kms to the journey. After leaving what was the main Accra road, the tracks were just sand and, as it was dry, it was easier than trying to drive on the tarmac. It was slow going and already almost half the day had been spent cushioning one's spinal cord on the rough terrain.

We eventually found Prampram and one landmark was the bow of a huge seagoing ship that had been washed up onto the shore in a typhoon in the past and left there, abandoned. It reared up over the tree-lined shore and dwarfed everything around it. I later walked along the beach to have a look at the vessel. The name was long obscured and there was no means of scaling its sides. It was an eerie place to be just standing near to this metal giant. A metal object was banging inside the hull and the wind hummed through the superstructure. All sorts of pictures flashed up in my mind—shipwreck, piracy, even a World War Two casualty, but the most likely answer was that the wild seas of the Gulf of Guinea had claimed this victim.

Prampram beach seemed to be used by brave and hardy souls who wanted to escape from Accra and Tema for a day out. As soon as we arrived beach traders appeared from nowhere with lobsters, prawns, exotic large shells and fruit available for very reasonable prices. We settled for a few lobsters and fruit and it was not long before the barbecue fire was in action. This rare treat was washed down with local beer and, for a short while, things were good.

I was not prepared for the next three hours, which I spent walking along the beach east towards Anloga. I heard screams and as I rounded the point where a river joined the sea there was a group of people gathered around a small body lying on the sand. A boy of about eleven years had got into trouble in the surf and was unconscious. I joined the wailing family and did my best to resuscitate the child, but he was gone. He had a nasty head wound that suggested the surf had smacked him down onto the seabed and then drawn him down with the undertow for which this coast was renowned. He was most probably unconscious before he drowned. There was little I could do. The family picked him up and carried him inland.

Not far away I encountered a net fisherman, fishing in the old style of casting a folded net into the river mouth and then retrieving it by pulling on two drawstrings to close the net's mouth and so entrapping the fish inside. The fisherman offered the nets to me but I declined. It would take a lot of practice to do this as easily as he. His catch consisted of small silver fish, similar to a perch at home. He had a bag on the ground and I saw that it was almost full. He had had a good day. "Chop fish," he said, and I nodded, shook his hand and wandered off.

Across the river mouth I saw the huts of a fishing settlement and decided that would be my turning point to return to my friends with a cold tin of beer. I was lucky; as I reached the village the entire community had just turned out to meet some fishing boats making their way in from the sea. They seemed to be almost sinking and wallowing in the waves and the surf. Ropes were thrown from the boats and grabbed by the women and old men in the surf and everyone began to pull them in. I could not believe my eyes! The boats were full to the brim with mackerel and the boatmen were literally standing in them, trying to keep their vessels upright in the waves. The mackerel were spilling over the sides of the boat because it was so full. I decided to join in and ran into the surf and grabbed a rope and began to pull. I was joined by about ten youngsters who all began to sing and pulled the rope to their rhythm. Six boats were pulled ashore with the largest quantity of mackerel I had ever seen. Not surprisingly, no one spoke English but, as the village was fairly isolated, we all got on famously.

After much handshaking and goodbye waves I was given six mackerel threaded onto a grass loop. I could not refuse such a gift as the barbecue would make good work of them. I returned slowly back along the shoreline quietly, thinking about the poor kid who had lost his life just playing at the seaside. I entered the only vegetation screen that came down almost to the water's edge and there was a well-trodden footpath through the bushes for about one hundred yards. I was alerted to sticks and twigs breaking on my right side but could not see anything and thought it was a bird or a monkey that I had startled. The noises came again and I looked for people who may be shadowing me but could see nothing. I felt a bit exposed, my only weapon being my Swiss army knife. I picked up a fairly solid wooden branch that would serve as a club if needed. Then I saw them—they were baboons! I did not know much about baboons except that they were large African monkeys that could be very belligerent if they wanted to be. There were four adults and some younger ones and they were on the same course as myself on a path that would join mine shortly.

They were making barking noises and were intimidating. My dilemma was should I risk joining them at the path junction, turn around, or go back, or what? We were fairly close now and I was not sure whether my wooden pole would be enough if they decided to have a go at me. Suddenly I realised it was not me they were after but my mackerel supper I was carrying. I decided to test the water by throwing one of the fish back behind them—and it worked! There was a rush to pick it up and a fur fight developed to see who ate it. I employed this diversionary tactic until I cleared the bush, throwing a fish at a time and then left them to it. My chums saw me coming back across the sand. "Interesting walk, Roy?" they asked. "What is that bit of grass you're carrying?" I sat down and took a swig from a beer tin. "Right guys, if you've got five minutes, listen to this!" I am not sure if they believed me, but that stroll has gone down in my memory as very eventful. It was the only time I had to enjoy the coastline, for my other visits were just a quick stop to buy fish from the roadside.

At the end of this day, I had the worst case of sunburn I have ever experienced. On each shoulder I had three almost open wounds that would need careful attention in this climate. They healed slowly and I gained the first freckles on my body as a result.

THE CHIEF'S PARTY

The day had arrived. It was a Friday and we would be finishing the training sessions at 3pm in order to be able to attend the Chief's party at Somania. The Chief had pressed us several times to visit his residence and our acceptance of his invitation was well overdue. I think that about twenty of our guards came from his principality and this was his way of saying thank you and welcome to Somania. We dressed formally, ensuring that we had long trousers and long sleeve shirts should there be an invasion of mozzies. Sarpong, who was driving, had also dressed for the occasion by donning his old beret and new trainers. The drive to the village was not long. I noticed the graveyard of derelict and abandoned East European tractors and the signs of fields cut in the bush that had returned to nature. The road was hard-baked sand and full of holes. The children kept filling in the holes with earth and then tried to get the travellers to pay a toll. Somania came into sight, a sprawling township with single storey buildings that had seen better days. There were roadside stalls selling tomatoes, onions, and I even saw a fresh dead monkey hanging from a pole. I hoped this would not appear on our menu that evening.

Sarpong wanted cigarettes so we stopped by a general store where there were bottles of all sorts, blocks of washing soap like those we used to have at school, plastic kitchen items and dozens of flip-flops made out of tyres. Whilst Sarpong purchased his fags I read the labels on the bottles. There was iodine in the standard green bottle, but years old. The label that really caught my eye was in a row of dusty medicine type bottles where the black writing on a white label said 'curls out'. This mixture apparently took out the natural curly hair of the African women who wanted straight hair like the rest of the world. There did not seem to be much of this liquid being sold. There were handwritten labels, baby love, brain vitalise, stomach doctor and sex change assistance! I could have stayed longer but we were late for the Chief.

The nearest way to describe the town centre is that it was like the centre of an English village with the green open space in the middle with the church in one corner and the Chief's home overlooking the area. There was no green grass, only hard-baked sandy soil and the village pond was a well where clean water came via a hand pump. It was a peaceful scene and despite Sarpong wanting to do a wheely, we approached slowly so as not to cause dust.

The Chief was waiting. He had erected umbrellas of banana leaves over tables and benches for our comfort and the beer was in front of us before we had a chance to sit down. I saw that the Chief was wearing his full ceremonial robes and a necklace and arm bracelet that was made of pure gold. We chatted about a hundred and one things. He was remarkably well informed—right up to date with European politics, and his claim to fame was that he had visited Crawley. The sun went down, bathing us in its orange reflection, and slowly the area became alive with visitors having a look at us. I heard the elders telling stories to the children about the white man whom they could now see in the flesh! Again we experienced the kids running up to us, pinching our skin on our arms and then running off shrieking with delight. The Chief eventually shooed them all away and we listened to the children signing a welcome song and using hand movements to illustrate their words. They were great.

Now it was time to eat. I had been aware that at the rear of the Chief's house there was a lot of activity and the smell of barbecue came over quite strong and also we were getting pretty hungry. The meal was served on a long table in front of us—rice, sweet potato, grilled fish, and salad which worried us since it may not have been washed except in the river water. The centrepiece was a large drum-like container, like a 50-gallon oil drum cut in half. This contained large pieces of meat and was steaming away. I think the main dish had been boiled in the drum and then left to steam dry leaving very little juice. The Chief dipped his hand into the pot and produced some pieces and offered them to us to eat. I became aware that we had to eat from the Chief's hand, as this was the height of good manners. I'm glad it was fairly dark by now as I did not want to examine the morsel in his hand too much, but I swear there was an eye in it. I let it slide down and made appreciative noises and thank God it was Paddy's turn. When the mood took the Chief he continued to dip and feed us as the evening went on. I was pleased when he gestured to the ladies that it was now their turn and they retired to the kitchen. Sweet was a mix of fruit that was acceptable. More beer flowed and I felt at ease but wondered if my stomach would hold together.

Dinner over, we laid back and watched the ladies dancing. They were easy on the eye, beautifully dressed. More singing and dancing followed by a mixed couple who enacted out a courting scene resulting in the bride's mother and father boxing the ears of the suitor and finally there was a happy ending. The beer flowed and the party went on. I remember being dragged onto the disco area by a large lady who twirled like a twenty-year-old. I thought, well, if I'm going to be ill maybe this will cure it. Paddy, despite much protesting, was suffering the same fate as I and, as you know, when you can't win you join the club. In the early hours of the morning we had danced ourselves to a point where we needed our rest. I signalled to Sarpong, who had watched two white men cavort like whirling dervishes, that we needed our overnight bags from the truck. I noticed he had lost his beret to a fairly plump lady who gazed adoringly at him and kept giggling.

"Who is that, Sarpong? Is she a friend?" He smiled. "A brother's wife—he is fishing." So be it. We thanked the Chief for his hospitality. He was a nice man with a great sense of humour, the extent of which I would soon learn to my cost.

The huts (perhaps that was a harsh word for them) were small guest single buildings with a bed, chair, table, washbowl, water and even a towel. I threw my bag down and took off my shoes and lay on top of the bed and I knew that it would not be long before I would crash out. Then I suddenly realised I was not alone. I grabbed my torch and, sure enough, there in the small annex corner were three young girls smiling at me as if I were on the menu.

"Sarpong, get in here!" I called. "Who are these ladies, and where did they come from?"

"From the Chief. He wishes you to have comfort. It is not good for a man to have a cold bed."

Bloody hell, I thought. What now? "Sarpong, more light. I want the girls to see something." I found my wallet and dug out my travelling photographs of Margaret and the family. "Look, I am married and I am in love with my family."

Sarpong looked very serious. "Mr Bishop—not for love but for friendship."

There is no answer to that really. Sarpong went on to enlighten me that to refuse the girls staying the night would not be good as they were the Chief's gift. I could hear noises from Paddy's accommodation and I am sure he was experiencing the same benevolent gesture. By now I was being got at by the three young ladies who seemed to think it was the done thing to disrobe a white man and examine his parts. I managed to regain some composure when I found the last of my Gatwick travel sweets and handed them over. This gave me a space to get some of my clothes back on. I knew this was going to be a long night. Maybe I could wait until they had fallen asleep before getting a nap. This was not to be, so the night passed in a form of wrestling in situations that I expect would be most men's idea of paradise. I really learned a great deal about these beautiful people and that the story that their pubic hair is like a brillo pad is not far from wrong. But I leave it to the reader to draw his or her own conclusions how I managed to survive the night.

In the morning the ladies departed with much giggling and promises that they would come to Akuse to visit us—God forbid, but it was well meant. Paddy emerged looking as if he had not slept a wink, but nonetheless honour on both sides was maintained. Sarpong chuckled all the way back to Akuse. I said to him: "The Chief was very generous, Sarpong—we must visit again." He looked sideways at me, not sure if I was joking. He said, "I have a friend in Atwa—he has many daughters. We visit him next time." I declined this kind offer and wondered if the jungle drums would broadcast our night out with the Chief?

THE WHITE BABY

Kingsley arrived at the bungalow at his usual punctual 6am, smart as always and carrying his plastic bag containing the standard hair brush, Bible and some small items of food. I constantly told him to help himself to the bread, sardines and marmite, but he always politely refused. He did however cook his own rations, which made me feel a little better. This morning I noticed he wanted to chat. Normally he was seen and not heard but today was different. I asked him how things were going and had he prayed for me recently. This normally kicked off some sort of exchange. I then thought that I saw a red glow underneath that ebony skin of his and he said, "In the village a white baby has been born." This was obviously the news of the year and I wondered it he thought it was mine. (It wasn't, I hasten to add—I knew that for sure!) I had to sit down and think this over.

The mother was Alice, the shop and barkeeper of the little rest stop on the Akuse-Somania crossroads not far away. Alice I knew well. Her small homemade dwelling with a tin roof was a stopping off point and a stop for the dozens of illegal taxis and trucks passing that way. Alice was a fine looking woman with prominent breasts that stood out at right angles from her body and certainly a sight to cheer up weary travellers and sex starved white expatriates. She sold bottled beer, always warm, and snacks which she said were turkey and chicken legs, but I doubted their real origin. Paddy ate there only once and had the worst case of the running bum I have ever witnessed. I was lucky that my cast iron stomach, as always, was keeping me in good stead. Many a man had made eyes at this lady because she was indeed quite beautiful and intelligent and would have graced any home in the UK (very well). One day I remember, when travelling back from Akosobo towards Alice's shack, I saw a white man in the bush off to my right and as I could not see a vehicle I stopped, thinking he might need help. When I reached him I saw he was not alone as he stood up with a young lady still entwined around his waist and, what do you know—it was Alice. They did not appear to be embarrassed. The guy I recognised as a water engineer from the Italian agency. He shouted, "Would you like some?" Alice waved her approval. I shouted, "No thanks, I'll leave you to it." I made a fairly quick departure and drove on to the watering hole. I saw that it was being looked after by Alice's brother who, when I asked if Alice was in, said she was visiting friends.

About one bottle of beer later the lovebirds turned up and I had two free turkey legs for my tea. The sums added up. Okay, I'm sure the baby was Antonio's but he had returned to Italy. This didn't seem to bother anyone. In fact, Alice was showing off her little girl at the beer bar to all and sundry. Life is amazing! In my travels I found that there were a number of babies of mixed race in Accra being born to Ghanaian men and East European women who had opted to live in Africa rather than the cold poverty-stricken lands at home. Most of the marriages did not last but they did produce in some cases almost white babies. I was to find that girls with very fair skin were highly valued and such a daughter would attract a high dowry from any prospective husband. No wonder Alice was happy. I was invited to 'the showing of the baby' ceremony, something like our baptism, I suppose. There was a Christian element to the procedure, but the old culture showed through which fascinated me. I was given lots of beer and lots of Ghanaian food (Ghana chop). We danced and listened to the drums and it was very, very acceptable. Alice's sisters were very naughty girls but Paddy and I managed to leave with our trousers still on.

THE DEAD MAN

Across the fields was Akuse Prison for low risk offenders, mainly thieves whom the judicial system had put there for their sins. I often saw a prisoner walking handcuffed across the footpath from the main road with the constable walking behind. There was no luxury of transport. I shudder to think how far this prisoner and escort had walked. Most low-level crime was dealt with by local tribunals rather than the police. In civil matters in the villages it was the paramount Chief who ruled on land disputes and domestic matters, including the complicated 'matrimonial' problems with unofficial wives. I found that the families of prisoners were responsible for their feeding and clothing, which you can imagine, would be a nightmare if the prison were miles away. Twice daily I saw women making their way to the prison. I had thought they were just visiting prisoners, but they were taking them their food.

The inside of a Ghanaian prison is not good. The message is *do not* do anything wrong or there is just a chance you could rot in one. This family responsibility extended to the few hospitals as well. If you were a patient, your family fed you, not the State. We do not know how lucky we are—or are we spoilt? The NHS needs to look at the family support system—it would save millions of pounds and discourage the malingerers!

It wasn't long before I experienced an incident where the family responsibility system left me in a quandary. One Tuesday I left the bungalow to travel to Akosombo for training. We had only gone a short way from Alice's beer shack when I saw a person lying at the side of the road and thought there might have been an accident, which was common, or perhaps it was just someone asleep. "Slow down, Sarpong!" I shouted, but he kept on going, shaking his head. "Not for us—it is a family problem."

I thought, okay, and for the remainder of the day tried to give it no further thought. On the return journey in the evening I saw that the 'body' was still there and, furthermore, that it was that of a man stark naked and covered in flies. "Stop, Sarpong!"—and this time he did. I covered my nose with my shirt and saw that there was indeed a large wound on the back of the head, which suggested he had been struck from behind by a vehicle. I noticed that Sarpong had not followed me but reversed away from the road. I waved Sarpong to join me and asked him to take me to the police post back on the Akosombo road. Sargong was agitated and said, "He is bala bala, he is crazy, there are bad spirits here." He persuaded me that he would report the matter to the police after dropping me off on his return to his home in Akosombo. I agreed with some doubt in my mind.

The following day, damn me, there was the body again and showing signs of putrefaction in the heat. I stopped the truck and said to Sarpong that I was going to the police. The police knew, he said, and still insisted that it was a family matter. Who will pay for the burial? I could see that this unfortunate corpse would never be buried, and it had to be done as animals had already eaten part of a leg. Back to the bungalow we went where I found an old bed cover. I soaked a small piece of cloth in the last of my aftershave, picked up what looked like a hoe or digging implement from the washroom, and went out to the truck. Sarpong had disappeared. I asked my bread lady if she had seen him and she said he was frightened. I returned to the corpse, which was in a hell of a mess. I tied my bit of cloth around my nose and spread out the bed cover alongside the body and with the branch of a tree I rolled the remains onto it. The stench was the worst I had smelt and I tried not to vomit. I dragged the body further back into the bush and found a spot with no trees or bushes and dug a grave. It was no more than what we would call a 'shell scrape' in the Army but it was all I could do in the hard ground. I dragged the body into the hole and covered what I could with the bed linen. It was no more than eighteen inches deep, but the poor sod was not very big. As you can imagine, once I had got the earth over the grave I felt a little better but the stink was still there. I piled rocks on top of the soil mound—quite a lot, in fact, because I was sure that some animal would try to dig it up. Finally I laid branches to camouflage the presence of a grave and, unless you looked very carefully, you could not see it from the roadside. I drove slowly back to the bungalow where I scrubbed up and had a shower (as usual in cold water) but I felt better. For the next week Sarpong did not sit with me in the truck, preferring instead to sit in the rear of the vehicle. I reported the grave to the police but they were just happy that the problem had been dealt with.

THE CHILDREN ARE SILENT

Before leaving the UK I had an occasion to visit the ferries at the Port of Dover as part of my Army resettlement training. Whilst there I met Commander Ted Sawkins, ex-Royal Navy, who was the Ship's Security Controller for Townsend Thoresson Ferries. Ted Sawkins was a great guy who knew what he was doing and did a good job. I mentioned to him that I was going off on a trip to Africa and he was most interested, being a well-travelled man himself. I jokingly said I would send him a postcard, not realising the mail difficulty I was to find. However, I did manage to find a postcard at Accra and I put it straight onto the mail plane, so it reached the UK. It was a car showing a very pretty Ghanaian girl in national costume and showing her best assets. I though he might enjoy that, being an old sailor. This was a good move on my part as Ted had decided to retire at about the same time as my contract finished in Ghana.

On my first visit home I went down to Dover and was interviewed by the directors, and obviously things went well as I was offered the appointment following Ted's retirement. The dates conflicted a little but this was an opportunity that could not be missed—and it was only fifteen miles from home.

When I returned to Ghana I waited for the exchange of formal letters before telling Paddy and my UK bosses about the job offer. I know that they were planning for me to remain for a further year as the contract was extended, but what do you do when things fall out of the sky? I was now faced with having to tell my colleagues and those African friends of whom I had become so fond. They obviously knew that the contract was not for ever, but nonetheless I felt like crap when I had to tell them the date I was going home. Kingsley started crying and burnt my shirt with the iron. Sarpong said nothing and washed the car, which was an event. My fishing chum Asamie said nothing and wandered off. What I could not get over to them was that it would have been time to go anyway.

Following the news I had announced, I came out of my bungalow the next morning and was struck immediately by the absence of any noise. Normally the children ambushed me at this time and we had our two minutes of greetings and chitchat, but today there was nobody. I saw Kingsley and asked, "What's happened, where is everybody?" He said, "The children are silent because you are going to England." I felt even worse now. On the trip down to the training school I even considered withdrawing my notice and continuing as we were because I felt I was letting them down. I decided to give myself a week and then see how my mind was at that time. After a week I had taken to the decision to take up my new job in Dover, but the thought that I had let them down remains with me even to this day. My friends, the little ones, came back into my daily routine but there was never that spontaneous shouting and clapping that we had enjoyed. I hope they learnt that the white man is not someone to be fearful of and that we are all in the end human beings.

Babs Wysocki, the wife of Alex, somehow had found a farewell card and spent time getting the friends and managers of the VRA to sign it and I have included a copy at the end of this book. Hopefully an attempt to read their messages will confirm a lot of what I have tried to convey to my reader. What you do in life echoes in eternity. This was my small contribution. There was a rash of people who came to me, seeking my UK address and telephone number. I gathered these were thought to be useful should they try to obtain visas, either to work in or visit the UK. I can't blame them—I certainly would have tried.

THE LAKE VISIT

During those last few days, I was given the opportunity to take a boat trip on the lake, which I had only really seen from the top of the dam. Alex Wysocki and I set off to drive to Ackosombo where his chum, the skipper of the presidential launch, was taking the vessel out for a test refit in Accra. The day was as hot as hell and there was no wind so, I thought, my landlubber's stomach would hold good. We met Hans at his bungalow and took coffee. He was already three parts pissed but a very easygoing man. He had found paradise with his sailing duties that were not arduous, and only on the occasions of state visits did he really have to concentrate on his sailing and his appearance.

The presidential launch was large and would have graced any port in the South of France. He had laid on cold beers and corned beef sandwiches and I stretched to view the passing land with one eye and tried not to fall asleep in this calm atmosphere. Hans gave me a call and pointed out basking Volta perch, some as big as a young man. He circled the small shoal and then pulled out a .22 rifle from a locker, eased back on the throttle and brought us within range of the fish. Two shots later and we were netting up two beautiful perch with enough fish meat to feed twenty people. He was going to donate them to the local fishing village where he had formed a relationship with a young lady who complemented his idyllic life.

We continued northwards until I spotted some workings on the western shore side. We gently eased our way alongside a makeshift jetty and were welcomed by a small group of German contractors who had a four month project to build a small port and three jetties to improve the shipping trade which flourished on the lake, bringing in mostly timber, vegetables, fruit and woven cloths from the upper regions of the Volta. The Germans were pleased to see us as they did not get any visitors in this isolated spot. The lunch they offered was one of the best I had eaten. Typically German, they were well organised and had their own refrigerated container stuffed full of good basic German foodstuffs—bratwurst sausages, meat balls, tinned fruit and vegetables, cream cakes and things I had not seen for a while. The lunch was washed down with Dortmunder Pilsner, which I had last seen when I was in Germany five years previously. It was very, very satisfying.

As we part-dozed in the sun after our lunch, I noticed a fairly large wooden vessel approaching the jetty and a small crowd had gathered to meet it. There were also some old lorries and small pickups, and I asked our host what the cargo was. He did not look very happy and suggested I should see for myself. I sauntered down to the lakeside and sat on a pile of timber watching the unloading. I had a shock when I saw there were literally thousands of smoked monkey carcasses being heaved ashore. They looked just like children and, even more disturbing, was the group of young children who were huddled together near the main cabin. There were no adults with them and I could not see any welcoming families on the shore. Hans had come down to join me and sat looking at the scene. He noticed I was getting agitated about the children and advised me not to ask questions. "The worst thing that is happening to them is that they will be put to work or married off. There is nothing you can do about it." That is the way it always has been and will remain so.

I saw the children being handed over to various people and put into the trucks. They were not crying but seemed to have accepted what was going on. Once the vessel had discharged its doubtful cargo it was then loaded with barrels of oil, building materials and domestic household items, all for resale in the north. It was time to leave our German hosts; theirs was a short contract and they would soon be on their way home.

Hans had got more drunk over lunch and on our return journey he decided to put his craft through some speed trials. I was pleased to see the top of the dam loom into sight and he eased back on our speed. We docked successfully, tied up and we made our way back to his bungalow. I noticed he had brought his .22 rifle with him—perhaps he was going to clean it! I was wrong. We sat in his garden in a semicircle, taking it in turns to nominate a target and try to hit it. After an hour there was a pile of bottled glass and punctured beer tins, which showed that our marksmanship wasn't too bad. The main problem was trying to keep Hans pointed in the right direction and not have a pot-shot at a neighbour he was not fond of.

Alex and I decided it was time to head for home. Hans had reached the head-nodding stage and his houseboy could ease him into his bed. It had been quite an interesting day so far. We decided to drive back to Akuse by a roundabout route, taking in a visit to a village where a local doctor advertised that he could undertake sex changes. Sure enough, I saw his sign advertising a variety of medical operations. We asked a passer by if he knew of any such operations being successful and he shook his head and informed us that only crazy people see this man.

Alex and I decided we would not have any consultations and continued our meandering to the next beer bar. There is something about losing oneself and you could certainly do that for a while. Mind you, there is no future in it, but who wants a future? We resisted the invitations to buy everything from onions to a goat and this time made our supreme effort to return to Akuse. My friendship with Alex and grown and I appreciated his companionship in this faraway place.

Epilogue

Now that the news of my departure was well known I had to hide my true feelings towards Africa and the effect it had had upon me. You either love or hate it. The continent is so vast that my personal feelings are confined to West Africa, as there are so many differing lands, in the North particularly. As I have said, you go around one corner and you are in paradise, around the next in hell, the colour of the soil, the immense space, the smell of the land and its people with life and death around you always. I am sure that if I had been born in Africa, these experiences and feelings may not have been so apparent; but to a time-expired soldier who had never served in this vast continent, it made a mark that cannot be erased.

I was misled by well meaning advisers who warned me that Africa can be your worst enemy. Trust no one and do not befriend anyone. They only want what is yours—what a load of bollocks! These short-sighted people overlooked the importance of communication, good manners, and the value of leading by example rather than by the adage, 'Don't do as I do, do as I tell you.' I have more respect for an African on his own ground than I do for a white man on his own ground.

The contract was ending; its popularity was high with no lack of volunteers to join the Volta River Authority, placing a heavy administrative burden upon the personnel department. The newly qualified security officers were now seen on duty. They are smart and efficient and in turn they are well looked after by their employer. The photographic proof I have provided shows what can be done with highly motivated men if they are given the chance.

I planned to hold a farewell party in the old Italian Clubhouse building. I knew that my friends had no money and I closed my bank account in Accra which left me with a pile of local currency which was no good in the UK for exchange purposes, so we decided to spend it all on a good cause. I cannot remember how much the bill was—very little in UK terms. We just enjoyed one another's company and everyone wanted to have their photograph taken. The power failed halfway through, but who cares—there are always candles and, anyway, this is Africa. You can expect a power cut now and then.

My fishing adviser Mr Boateng was in tears. He could only take three beers as he did not drink. I had donated my telescopic long rod and all of my fishing kit to him. He was probably the only man in Ghana with such modern kit, though I don't think this guaranteed he would catch anything. The old ways are sometimes the best methods. He had lost his friend who would not be feeding his family anymore, and he was not a happy fisherman. I shall not forget his loyalty on occasions when the chips were down.

At the end of a jolly evening I remember writing out my last Chartered Bank of Ghana cheque and giving it to Eddie Dzienyo, the Club Manager, and to this day that cheque has never been cashed. The last few days passed in a whirl. I gave my remaining foodstuffs to Paddy: there was some doubtful pork chops, tins of beans and little else. Kingsley had gone broody and was saying nothing. He quietly got on with his few chores and was obviously very worried about his future, though I had thought of that. I paid him the equivalent of four months' wages from my mass of local money. He was so pleased he said he would have to bury it, as it was so much. At least I know he was now *au fait* enough to find a job, perhaps in Accra with a white family, having looked after me well, even though I was not a demanding person.

I gave my driver Sarpong two months' wages, which disappeared into his pocket as if it was Christmas. He said he was going to have another wife and that this would help him. For the guys in the training office I had already bought them watches and shoes for their wives on my previous trip home. It was not easy as I thought, just picking up a suitcase and getting into the truck outside the bungalow.

As we drove away I wanted to look around but did not. As we turned left on the main road for Akuse I stopped the pickup and shouted at Krobo Hill—this place with its patient people, with its hardships, this place with really nothing, had got to me.

The last night was spent in Accra with us bedding down at the guesthouse. There was time for a quick trip to a nearby hotel for a final beer. The hangers-on must have thought I was crazy, as I still had quite a bit of local money left. It was drinks all around for a while, leaving just enough for the mandatory tips at the airport the next day. I passed through the controls, giving money away, and when I reached the final checkpoint it was the Special Branch guys who asked, "Any Cedis you won't need, Mr Bishop?" and I could then say, "Sorry, nothing."

Aboard the British Caledonian flight I spent Mum's last £10 note that I had kept hidden in my shoe. After three whiskies I thought over my stay and knew that it had made an impact on me that would remain with me always. I knew that

I now believed that Africa was for the Africans but, at the same time, there is no need to scoff at the role of the white man in independent countries. Far from it. Until there have been more advances in education, industry and administration, the white man is very valuable, though not indispensable. Europeans will be necessary until all the technical and administrative skills are learnt. Without risking too much, I should say that Africans have a poor instinct for business, as trading traditionally has been in the hands of Indians, Levantines, Arabs and Portuguese.

In Ghana there is much evidence that key industries are now being run by Ghanaians, and most efficiently. For me I could feel the beginning of a restlessness that had come about by learning the truth about myself. To the white people who live there, the idea of Africa is an obsessional thrill and addiction. Africa was once known as the white man's grave. There is some mysticism. They feel that back there, somehow, there is the truth about the beginning of life. I agree with these thoughts. I hope the reader of my tale will not think that I have gone bush happy. At the time of writing this story all that I forecast has been confirmed. I have since returned to this remarkable continent seeking whatever it is that prompts me to do so. I hope to relate some of my findings in due time.

Having been home for a while, my thoughts constantly dwelt on my stay in Ghana. Some days I missed it and some days I did not. Stuck in a traffic jam on the M25 on a hot summer's day, or being pressured by boy racers on the Ashford ring road, certainly made me yearn for the wide open spaces and the slow pace of life of the people; but, then, whilst sitting in the local curry restaurant consuming a tasty meal washed down with a glass of cool beer, I was content.

The odd Christmas card arrived from Africa. They took a long time to reach me but were appreciated. It was interesting to note that in the pictured nativity scene the baby Jesus, his parents and the three wise men were all black Africans. I wonder how close to the truth this really is? What really made my day was when I received a telephone call from Alex Wysocki. He and his wife were on their way to Canada via the UK to visit Barbara's relatives in Essex, and they were coming to Ashford to visit me and deliver some letters of goodwill. I met them in the County Hotel in the town centre and there they were—brown and healthy and carrying a cardboard box, a gift for me from the people of Akuse. "What is it?" I enquired. "They said open it—we've had to carry it all the way as hand luggage!"—and there it was, an earthenware red soil cooking pot made from the ground in Akuse. I was delighted and I am sure those sitting near us in the bar did not understand why a mature white man was so pleased with a pot.

The pot now stands in my garden as one of my most treasured possessions. I've turned it upside down and placed it in a protected corner; as far as anyone is concerned, it contains my lucky 'Ju Ju' spirit that will, at some time, bring me good luck.

Sure enough, life has been good to me. My family members are in good health and we enjoy a secure existence. The fact that I have attempted to record my experiences in Africa in this story and express my personal views demonstrates how I feel. I am a better man for this journey in time.

I cannot, actually, wait for my next opportunity to continue my learning curve in my new adopted continent. I have an offer for employment in Senegal. Should I go?

Epilogue 125

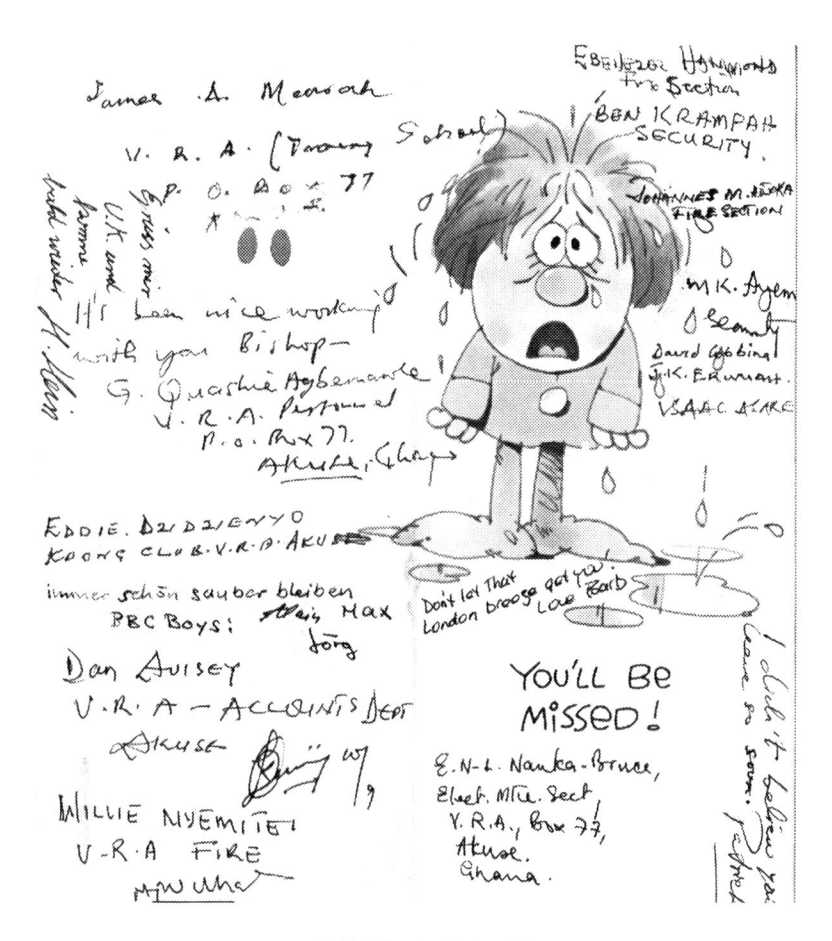

MY 'GOOD-BYE' CARD!

On the reverse side are many more messages, including that of Alex Wysocki who wrote:
"Bish—May All your Kindness be repaid in Life."

978-0-595-32538-2
0-595-32538-6

Lightning Source UK Ltd.
Milton Keynes UK
03 November 2009

145790UK00001B/107/A